The Magician's Dream
(an Oona Crate Mystery: book 3)

Shawn Thomas Odyssey

Oona Crate Mysteries

The Wizard of Dark Street (book 1)
The Magician's Tower (book 2)
The Magician's Dream (book 3)
—

Also by Shawn Thomas Odyssey

The Monster Society

—

All books available as audiobooks from
audible.com

—

For my friends.

I could not ask for better.

Prologue

An excerpt from the *Encyclopedia Arcanna*

DARK STREET (a.k.a. Little London Town):
Dark Street is the last of the original thirteen Faerie roads that connect the World of Man to the enchanted Land of Faerie. A world unto itself, the thirteen-mile-long street exists between the massive Iron Gates at the north end and the Glass Gates at the south.

Like the hour hand on a clock, Dark Street rotates, moving through the space between worlds—a space known as the Drift. At the stroke of midnight, the street stops and the Iron Gates open upon New York City. The gates remain open for exactly one minute before closing again so the street may once more begin its rotation.

At the opposite end stand the Glass Gates, which lead to the Land of Faerie, and have remained closed since Oswald the Great locked them shut in the year 1313, thereby ending the horrendous thirteen-year Great Faerie War.

In the very center of Dark Street—where the cobblestoned avenue splits apart in a wide circle—sits Pendulum House, an enormous enchanted manor house with a crooked tower poking precariously from its many slanted roofs, and the prow of an ocean-faring ship jutting out of the second floor like the remains of a sea wreck. It is here, at number 19 Dark Street, that the Wizard and his apprentice make their home. If the Glass Gates should ever fall, it is the Wizard's job to protect Dark Street, New York City, and the World of Man from a faerie attack.

Chapter One

The Forest of Books
(Tuesday, December 18, 1877)

"It is time to begin your battle training," said the Wizard.

"Battle training?" Oona asked.

"To prepare you."

"For what?"

"Battle!"

Oona glanced at Deacon to see if the bird understood what her uncle was talking about. Grim and composed, Oona's raven companion flexed his talons upon her shoulder. The firelight reflected off his long black feathers, which he rustled slightly but otherwise gave no indication that he understood the Wizard's meaning.

The two of them stood before the dragon-bone desk in the Wizard's study. The sides and top of the desk rose and fell in steady waves, as if the bones were sleeping, lost in a dream. Tall, intricately carved bookshelves covered the back wall, the grimy spines of the books looking cracked and worn. Near the fireplace, a teacup floated several inches above a side table as if caught on a current of warm air. It moved in an endless crazy-eight pattern, its handle dusty, its contents long ago evaporated.

Oona raised one eyebrow at Uncle Alexander.

He read her expression well. "I am quite serious, Oona. There may come a day, after you have taken over the position of Wizard of Dark Street, that the Glass Gates fall. It is a possibility that every Wizard must prepare for, no matter how unlikely it is to happen. Because if the gates do fall, and Dark Street is open to the Land of Faerie, then it would be your responsibility to tap into the magic of Pendulum House and to protect not only Dark Street against a faerie invasion but also all of New York and the World of Man beyond."

Oona frowned. "You know, I dislike that term, Uncle."

"The term?"

"World of Man."

The Wizard shook his head. "I do not understand. That is what it is called. What is there to not like?"

Deacon cleared his throat. "She means that she does not like the use of the word *man*."

"But it is a fitting description," the Wizard reasoned. "It is the world where men have ruled and lived for centuries."

Oona's mouth flattened into a straight line. "Not just men, but also women. And boys. And girls."

The Wizard pressed his pipe to his lips and puffed. He leaned back, nodding thoughtfully. "And what would you suggest?"

"The World of Humans," Oona said.

The Wizard looked inquisitively at Deacon.

Deacon clacked his beak before answering: "Don't look at me. I didn't put the idea into her head."

"Certainly not," Oona said. "Deacon would have us call it the World of Birds."

"There are more birds in the World of Man than there are men, women, and children put together," Deacon said wisely.

"Yes, well, Deacon would know that, wouldn't he?" said the Wizard.

Her uncle was referring to the fact that the raven was not only gifted with the ability to speak, but he also had an impressive number of books stored in his head, including the entire *Encyclopedia Arcanna*, an extensive set of reference books containing texts on nearly all things magical.

Oona looked from Deacon to her uncle, her jaw jutting out in frustration. Neither of them was taking her seriously. It was infuriating.

"Let me guess," the Wizard said. He puffed several times on his pipe and then exhaled a cloud of smoke that formed into a woman's face. The likeness of the smoky face to that of their new housemaid was astonishing. "You got this idea from our new cleaning maid: Mrs. Carlyle."

Oona's frown deepened. Why did her uncle think it unlikely that she had come up with the idea on her own? Did he think she did not see the inequality between men and women in their society? Of course, what he had suggested was true, their new housemaid had indeed introduced her to the idea of discrimination against women. Mrs. Carlyle had many progressive ideas, especially those about women's rights, which Oona found fascinating.

Oona had come to appreciate the presence of another female in their house. Even if they could not afford a full-time live-in maid, it was still pleasant to have the house cleaned on a daily basis. Pendulum House may have been instilled with immense magical powers, but the Magicians of Old—who had created the house nearly five centuries ago, as a home for the first official Wizard—had not implemented any self-cleaning spells. There were rooms Oona did not dare enter for fear of stirring up layers of ancient dust or getting tangled in a labyrinth of cobwebs.

But more than having a clean house, it was Mrs. Carlyle's intelligent and well-informed conversation that had inspired Oona in the month since the maid had been hired. Still, it irked Oona to know that her uncle believed her incapable of having such ideas of her own.

—

She gave the Wizard a severe look. "You know, there is a *woman* running for a seat on the Dark Street Council this year."

"I do know," the Wizard said. "Molly Morgana Moon has threatened to run for more than ten years. She seems an ideal candidate. It's too bad she won't win."

Oona's hands dropped to her hips. "How can you know that? Voting day is still four days away."

Deacon clicked his beak before uttering: "He knows because Mrs. Moon is running against Tobias Fink, the current council member...a suspected associate of Red Martin."

"So?" Oona said.

"So," Deacon continued, "he has all of Red Martin's considerable wealth to help him win votes."

"To help him *bribe* votes would be more accurate," the Wizard said.

Deacon nodded agreement.

Oona shook her head in disgust. Red Martin, the ultra reclusive owner of the Nightshade Hotel and Casino, was the infamous head of the Dark Street criminal underground. Despite the fact that he was wanted on a stack of criminal charges, including masterminding a plot to imprison the Wizard, it was known that Red Martin had many of the Dark Street Council members in his pocket.

"But Red Martin is wanted by the police," Oona said. "He is in hiding."

"But he is still in charge," the Wizard said. He let out another cloud of smoke, this time obscuring his face and body completely, his hands poking through the smoke like those of a puppeteer. "He's running things from behind the scenes, just as he always has. And also, if you ask me, I'm afraid that the voters are not ready to vote for a female politician." The Wizard held up a hand as Oona opened her mouth to protest, and then waved the smoke away. "I know—it is ridiculous. I, myself, will be voting for Molly

Morgana Moon because I believe in the principles she stands for: a crackdown on crime and more money for literacy and education. Yet I can't help but wonder, is Dark Street ready to vote for a female council member when it has been only ten years since women gained the right to vote here?"

Oona's eyebrows shot up in surprise. "Only ten years ago?"

"That is correct," the Wizard said. He removed his wand from his pocket and pointed it toward the window. An image appeared on the glass of a woman in a jail cell. "And outside the Iron Gates, in New York City and the world beyond, women still do not have the right to vote."

"It is true," Deacon said in his matter-of-fact tone. "Only a few years ago, a woman by the name of Susan B. Anthony was the first woman to vote in a United States presidential election...but she was arrested for doing so because it was illegal, and was put on trial for it."

The Wizard lowered his wand, and the image of the woman in the jail cell faded away.

Oona's fingers pressed into her palms. It was beyond frustrating to learn that, in the modern age of 1878, women were still treated as if their thoughts and opinions were not important. She wondered what could be done about it.

The Wizard smiled at her, and his smile made her even more cross. How could he be so amused by this injustice?

Once again he held up his hand, as if warding off her thoughts. "I was just thinking that you remind me of your mother. She was on the forefront of the fight to gain women the right to vote here on Dark Street."

Oona was taken by surprise. She had not known this about her mother. She was both elated and saddened to learn of it; elated because she had secretly hoped her mother would have been proud of Oona's interest in women's rights, but saddened because her mother was not alive to share in it.

Oona could feel the guilt and loss begin to rise up within her, and rather than pursue the matter, she changed the subject.

"You were saying...about battle training?"

The Wizard leaned forward, his long gray beard wafting above the desk. "Ah, yes. The training. There will be four days of tests, consisting of various magical challenges that you must overcome. They will be quite difficult, I assure you. And then on the fifth day you will face a sort of ancient rite of passage: a challenge that will require all of the magical skills you have been tested on in the previous days. The first test will begin today, at three o'clock. Here in the house."

"Today?" Oona said, startled. "But..."

"But what?"

"I was planning on visiting the new library today."

The Wizard exhaled another cloud of pipe smoke and peered at her through one eye. "Weren't you just there yesterday?"

Deacon cleared his throat. "And the day before that."

Oona's face flushed red. "Yes, well, I have a lot of reading to do."

Deacon tutted and Oona was tempted to nudge him off her shoulder. Deacon knew her true reason for visiting the new library so often, and she could only hope that he would keep his beak shut about it.

She cleared her throat. "It really is a marvel, Uncle. The new library, I mean. It's so much larger than the old one."

The Wizard nodded thoughtfully. "Of course, we have one of the finest *private* libraries on the street right here in Pendulum House. Certainly the greatest *magical* library this side of the Glass Gates. No need to venture out." He squinted at Oona through a plume of smoke. "Unless, of course, your fascination with the new library has to do with something other than books."

Oona did her best to restrain her grin. "Why, I can't imagine what you mean, Uncle. Why else would I wish to visit the library?"

—

7

"Three o'clock. That gives us six hours to prepare for the battle training."

Oona and Deacon moved purposefully down the Pendulum House hallway. Beneath Oona's feet, the carpet changed color with each step, while the wallpaper kept pace with her stride, its squiggly Victorian patterns moving like swarms of swimming jellyfish.

"What do you imagine the test will consist of?" she asked.

"I'm sure I have no idea," Deacon replied.

Oona came to an abrupt halt, the shapes in the wallpaper crashing into one another as she did so. It was unlike Deacon not to know something about the magical world.

"You mean to say there is nothing in the *Encyclopedia Arcanna* about these battle tests? According to Uncle Alexander, every Wizard's apprentice has had to go through them."

Deacon nodded. "That is precisely what I am saying. It would seem that the Wizards have purposefully kept such secrets...well...secret. That is to say, out of public knowledge. The *Encyclopedia Arcanna* is public information. Anyone with a library card can have access to it, so there is no information there to be had."

A heavy weight seemed to drop into Oona's stomach, and she knew it was not from her breakfast. It was anxiety, and that kind of anxiety usually came from one thing: not knowing something that she needed to know.

Sensing her frustration, Deacon added: "There are many other sources on magic in the Pendulum House library, *secret* books not available to the general public. Perhaps we could find something there."

—

8

Oona snapped her fingers, and the squiggling patterns in the wallpaper scattered like retreating insects. "That is no doubt why Uncle Alexander mentioned the house's private library. He was giving me a clue. Come, Deacon, let us unravel this mystery and prepare for battle."

She arrowed a finger and began to march down the hallway, followed by a procession of squiggly wallpaper patterns, all marching in sync to Oona's decisive stride.

They entered the library to the sound of giggling. At first Oona could not tell where the sound was coming from. Unlike a normal library, which would usually be composed of straight walls and shelves filled with books, the Pendulum House library gave the impression that one was entering a lush forest.

Thick trunked trees grew out of the floor and up the crooked walls, their branches and limbs holding what must have been thousands of leather-bound books, most of which looked so old and untouched that they had become part of the trees themselves.

One of the biggest rooms in the house, it was an easy place in which to get lost. The forest of books twisted and turned, with tables fashioned out of knobby tree roots and large spotted mushrooms for seats. Countless vinelike ladders gave access to the books above.

Dozens of lighted orbs floated near the high ceiling, casting their enchanted light down through the branches in broken rays. Yet as fascinating as the library was, finding a book in the chaos was a daunting task. As far as Oona knew, there was no logical system or order to it. Samuligan, the house faerie servant, was the only one who seemed to understand its chaotic organization.

"Do you hear that?" Oona asked Deacon.

The giggling started up again, as if coming from deep within the forest.

"I do," Deacon replied.

Oona stepped over several roots and ducked beneath a low-hanging branch. The deeper she ventured, the louder and more distinct the sound became. Rounding the thick-bottomed trunk of a book-laden oak, they came upon Mrs. Carlyle. The maid stood precariously upon one of the vine ladders and was dusting a bookshelf branch with one of the Wizard's enchanted feather dusters. Each time the feathers tickled a shelf or book, the duster would begin to giggle uncontrollably in the maid's hand.

"Hello, Mrs. Carlyle," Oona said.

The maid let out a startled yelp and nearly fell from her ladder. One of the books flew from the branch and nearly collided with Oona's head.

"Oh, dear," Oona said, and reached out, meaning to break the maid's fall. But the maid caught her balance at just the last moment. Oona stared up at her, wide-eyed. "Are you all right?"

The maid threw a hand to her chest and let out a sigh. "Oh, it's you, Miss Crate. My, did you ever give me a fright."

"I'm sorry. I didn't mean to startle you."

"Oh no, it's not your fault," Mrs. Carlyle said as she climbed shakily down from the ladder. "I thought you might be that other."

"Other?" Deacon asked.

"I think she means Samuligan," Oona said.

"Aye, so I do," Mrs. Carlyle replied. "Gives me the willies, he does."

She looked nervously around, as if Samuligan might be lurking among the books in a nearby tree. A thin woman in her late forties, Mrs. Carlyle's large round eyes and high cheekbones gave her the appearance of a skittish squirrel. She fidgeted nervously with her bonnet and then smoothed the apron of her black-and-white maid's uniform.

Oona wished to put her at ease. She truly appreciated having another female in the house and hoped that Samuligan would not frighten off Mrs. Carlyle.

"Oh, don't mind Samuligan," Oona said reassuringly. "You'll soon get used to him."

Mrs. Carlyle shook her head. "I'm thinking probably not. Keeps popping out at me, all over the house. Asking if I need help, and then before I know it, he's got the dishes flying about the ceiling like a flock of doves, or might be the table I'm dusting suddenly goes floating upside down, and me with it! I don't like it, let me tell you. I get motion sickness, so I do. This here forest seems to be the only place I've managed to avoid him."

It's only a matter of time, Oona thought, but knew better than to share it out loud.

"I'll have a word with him," Oona said, though in truth she knew that much of the magic that happened in Pendulum House was not due to the faerie servant.

Deacon, who appeared to be having a similar train of thought, said: "Not all of the unnatural occurrences are due to Samuligan. Pendulum House is steeped in magic, and many of the house's peculiarities come from the random surfacing of the ancient power it holds. Nearly five hundred years ago, the Magicians of Old combined their remaining magic and placed it into the house. They then chose a custodian of that magic—a keeper known as the Wizard."

Mrs. Carlyle ran a thumb across her feather duster, causing it to giggle several times. "All's I know is that whenever that faerie's around, funny things start to happen."

The maid bent down to retrieve the fallen book. "Look at that. The strangest books you have in here."

The book had fallen open to a page revealing a drawing of a large, hairy creature with the body of a man and the head of a bull.

"It is a minotaur," Deacon said. "And that book is a

rare copy of *Mortenstine's Monstrous Conspectus*. Possibly the only copy left in existence. Please do be careful." Mrs. Carlyle peered at the creature and visibly shivered. "Sure would hate to come across him out on the street, so I would."

Oona peered at the image and had to agree. "I looked through *Mortenstine's Conspectus* several years back...and I had bad dreams for a week. I remember that minotaur was exceptionally vicious."

"He's not real, is he?" the maid asked.

Deacon, who seemed to have no interest in putting the maid at her ease, said: "He is."

The maid appeared truly alarmed.

Oona threw Deacon a scornful look. "Yes, he is...but what Deacon neglected to say was that no minotaur has been seen this side of the Glass Gates for hundreds of years. Nor most of the other creatures in that book."

She reached over and closed the book in the maid's hands before attempting to change the subject. "Will you be attending Mrs. Molly Morgana Moon's campaign rally on Wednesday?"

"I will if your uncle will give me the time off. Takes place in the middle of the day, and those are my usual work hours."

Oona was surprised. "What do you mean if Uncle Alexander will give you the time off? Of course he will. We can go together. After all, I might not have known about the rally if you hadn't told me it was happening."

Mrs. Carlyle smiled. "That's good of you, Miss Crate. But don't go making trouble."

"Trouble?" Oona asked. "What do you mean?"

Mrs. Carlyle sighed. "It's just that most householders would not let their servants attend such functions during work hours...and I do need this job. So please, if he insists I stay here and do my work, don't argue with him. I can support women's rights on Saturday, when I vote."

12

Oona opened her mouth to protest, but seeing the concerned look on Mrs. Carlyle's face, she realized that as much as the maid was concerned for women's rights, she was also concerned for her job. Oona didn't think the Wizard would mind; after all, they had gone over half a year with no maid at all, and he himself was a supporter of Molly Morgana Moon's politics. But rather than drive the point home, Oona once more steered the conversation to a less-upsetting subject.

"I see you are using one of the enchanted dusters."

"Oh, this," Mrs. Carlyle said, frowning. "I forgot my own at home, so I grabbed this one from the cleaning cupboard. It keeps laughing at me."

"It's not laughing at you," Oona explained. "It's just very ticklish. It's one of the novelty objects my uncle sells in his enchantment shop...though it's not one of his most attractive creations. It's not exactly a best seller."

"I can see why," Mrs. Carlyle said, and then smiled. "Speaking of attractive, how's that young Mr. Iree?"

Oona's face grew suddenly warm. "Oh, he's...he's just fine. At least he seemed so the last time I spoke with him."

"And when was that?" Mrs. Carlyle asked.

Oona grinned. "Yesterday."

"Really?" Mrs. Carlyle said, feigning surprise. "I must hear all about it."

Deacon cawed loudly from Oona's shoulder. "I'm sorry, Mrs. Carlyle, but Miss Crate has some research to do, so if you don't mind—"

"There's no need to be rude, Deacon," Oona snapped, and she felt a sudden wave of embarrassment. This was one of the reasons it was so nice to have another female in the house. As much as she loved Deacon and her uncle, and Samuligan, too, there were just certain things she could not talk to them about.

Deacon rustled his feathers uneasily. "But your first battle test is at three o'clock. That gives us little enough time to research as it is."

Mrs. Carlyle continued to smile fondly at Oona, as if she had not heard a word Deacon had said. "I must have been about your age when I first met the boy who would grow up to be my husband: Mr. Carlyle. Even back then I knew he was the one, because—"

"I'd say, that's quite enough!" Deacon squawked. "And I'd ask you, Mrs. Carlyle, to please stop putting ideas of matrimony into Miss Crate's head. She is far too young to be thinking of such things, and she has very important magical research to do. Now please return to your duties."

"Deacon!" Oona half shouted.

She was suddenly furious. Not just because Deacon was being so rude to Mrs. Carlyle, but because he had interrupted her just when the maid was going to tell her how she knew that her husband had been *the one*. Oona desperately wanted to know what the clue had been.

Mrs. Carlyle turned abruptly to the ladder and began to climb back to the branch she had been dusting. "Oh no, Mr. Deacon's quite right. If you have research to do, I shouldn't be getting in your way." She stopped halfway up the ladder and turned. "Then again, there are other places to do research that you might find more...informative."

"Don't be ridiculous," Deacon said. "The Pendulum House library contains Dark Street's most rare magical texts. Indeed, I believe it is safe to say that it houses perhaps the most obscure books written about magic in all of the World of Man."

"World of *Humans*," Oona corrected him.

Mrs. Carlyle gave her a wink.

Deacon sighed. "Regardless, many of these books are one of a kind. Where else would we find information on your apprenticeship battle training?"

But Oona understood that Mrs. Carlyle was not necessarily referring to information about apprentice battles, and that she was more than likely suggesting that Oona could

14

find the answers she was seeking about *the one* somewhere else—like, for instance, a place where a certain tattoo-faced boy happened to be working as a shelving assistant. Somewhere like...

"The new public library," Oona said.

Deacon shook his head. "It is highly unlikely that the *public* library will possess any information if the *Encyclopedia Arcanna* has none to offer. I suggest we find a book here. We should call for Samuligan's assistance."

"Yes, you are right, Deacon," Oona said, before shouting: "Samuligan!"

"You called?" came the silky, sly voice from above.

Mrs. Carlyle screamed in surprise, dropping the duster and slipping down several rungs on the ladder. The duster continued giggling like a loon as it tumbled through the air, letting out a loud honk of laughter upon hitting the floor. Samuligan's long face poked out from between two sets of books in the exact place the maid had been dusting. He grinned his horrible smile—a smile that showed too many teeth.

It took Oona a moment to understand what she was looking at, and then she realized that the branch that the maid had been dusting had not been a branch after all, but was actually Samuligan, who was wrapped in his dusty old cloak and sticking bizarrely out of the side of the tree.

He sat up, the books toppling to the floor, and Mrs. Carlyle hurriedly scurried down the ladder to hide behind Oona. The faerie's long jacket had been transformed into the same dark brown texture as the bark of the tree, but as he hopped to the library floor, the coat once again took on its normal shade of midnight black.

The faerie servant, who stood nearly six and a half feet tall, tipped his black cowboy hat at Mrs. Carlyle. The maid gave a little whimper from behind Oona.

"Now, Samuligan, that was not very nice," Oona said. "You startled Mrs. Carlyle."

15

"My apologies," Samuligan said, though he did not sound too apologetic. Oona knew this was the best she could expect from him. There would be time to speak to him about his behavior later. For now she needed to hurry if she was going to get in all she wanted to do in the day before her first battle test at three o'clock.

"Samuligan, we need to find a book," Deacon said.

"Yes, we do," Oona said quickly, before the faerie could respond. "So please…bring around the carriage. We're off to the public library."

Deacon groaned.

Chapter Two

The Faerie Carbuncle

"Bizarre," Deacon said.

"You say that every time we come here," Oona said.

"I can't seem to help it," Deacon replied.

Oona stepped from the carriage and craned her neck back. Above them, built directly on top of the enormous stone fortress that was the Museum of Magical History, the new public library towered over the street looking like a battered old witch's hat. Four stories tall, the building coned to a floppy point as it rose toward the purplish-blue sky. The brim of the hatlike structure drooped over the edges of the museum like sagging cloth, while a stone hatband displayed the words PUBLIC LIBRARY in letters carved a full story tall.

"According to the *Dark Street Tribune*," Deacon added, "this was the only place big enough to host the new facility."

"The design is supposed to celebrate the magical heritage of the street," Oona said as she started up the stone steps toward the museum door.

"Looks more like someone left their hat out in the rain," Deacon said.

Oona laughed. "Someone with a bigger head than you?"

"Me?" Deacon quipped. "I'm not the one who thinks I can pass a magical battle test unprepared."

Oona pulled open the museum door and stepped through. "Who says I'm going to be unprepared? There's plenty of time to—"

Oona came to an abrupt halt in the entryway. Composed of tall curving walls and a high beamed ceiling, the room was home to an awe-inspiring circle of enormous monolithic stones—an exact copy of Stonehenge in England, except unlike their English counterparts, these stones had been perfectly preserved. The museum was a seldom-visited place, and more often than not, the tall gray stones stood stark and lonely.

But today the entryway was a bustle of activity. Along with the usual museum guard, three police constables occupied the circle of stones, as well as what looked like a second museum guard whom Oona did not recognize. One of the police constables, a tall man with a potbelly and arms that seemed too long for his body, stepped to one side, revealing two more people.

The first was the museum curator, Mr. Glump, a short man with a neatly trimmed beard and pointy nose. Oona had once questioned him about a pair of magical daggers that had been stolen from the museum. If she remembered correctly, the curator had had a streak of bad luck while gambling at the Nightshade Casino.

The second person Oona saw was none other than Inspector White, the tall, extremely pale-faced man who had taken over Oona's father's position as head of the Dark Street Police Department after her father had been killed in the line of duty. Inspector White was speaking very animatedly to the second museum guard—the one Oona did not recall having seen before. Oona's heart began to thrum, and a tingle of excitement raced up her arms.

18

"It appears to be some sort of crime scene," Deacon said, and then quickly added: "Perhaps we should come back later."

"Later?" Oona scoffed. "But look, Deacon. It is a case."

"I was afraid you might say that," Deacon replied. "But don't you think we should head back to the Pendulum House library to research your tests?"

But Oona was already approaching the first museum security guard, who happened to be the closest person to her. A thickset man in a gray uniform, the guard did not seem to notice her approach, but when Oona tapped him on the arm, he jumped nearly an inch off the floor.

"What? Huh? What?" He glanced around looking confused before settling his gaze upon Oona and Deacon.

"Hello," Oona said.

"The museum is closed," the guard said, "but the library upstairs is open, if you wish."

He gestured toward the stairs that had been built along the curved wall.

"What has happened here?" Oona asked.

The guard eyed her suspiciously, looking as if he were about to tell her to mind her own business. He glanced in the direction of Inspector White, who was now speaking with Mr. Glump. After a moment's consideration, the guard shrugged and spoke in a half whisper.

"Break-in."

Oona's eyes widened. "Someone broke into the museum?"

The guard nodded toward the man in the circle of stones who, like himself, was dressed in a museum guard's uniform. The unknown man was rubbing at his wrists and listening to the conversation between Inspector White and Mr. Glump. "That's Elbert Hackelsmith. He's the night watchman. I found him all tied up there in the circle of stones this morning. Tied good and tight. I had to cut the rope to get him out."

He gestured toward the tangle of white rope that lay in the center of the room.

"What was stolen?" Oona asked.

The guard once again glanced in the inspector's direction before answering in a hushed tone: "The Faerie Carbuncle."

Deacon gasped, but Oona only shook her head. She had never heard of it.

"What's a carbuncle?" she asked.

"It's none of your business, Miss Crate," said a high, irritating voice.

Oona turned to discover Inspector White striding in her direction. His long black coat wafted about his lanky legs as his impossibly white face pinched into a dissatisfied scowl.

"Hello, Inspector," Oona said. She smiled in an attempt to put him at his ease.

"Don't 'hello' me, Miss Crate. This is a crime scene. And what have I told you about crime scenes?"

Oona placed a finger to her lips, as if trying to remember. "Hmm, let's see. You mean the bit about not interfering with an ongoing police investigation?"

The inspector shook his finger at her. "Don't get smart with me."

Oona frowned. "*You* asked the question. I simply answered."

"But you should not be answering at all, Miss Crate, because you should not even be here." He paused for a moment, rubbing at his ghostly chin before adding: "Not unless you had something to do with the theft of the carbuncle."

Oona had to work hard not to roll her eyes. "I don't even know what a carbuncle is."

Deacon rustled his feathers and spoke from her shoulder, expounding upon his encyclopedic knowledge of

20

the magical world. "A carbuncle is a large cut gemstone, usually red, and highly valuable. In this case, the stolen object appears to be the infamous Faerie Carbuncle, an enchanted ruby attached to a golden necklace. It is purported to give the person wearing the necklace the same extraordinary magical powers as a faerie, provided the wearer recites the ancient incantation that activates it. But the activation spell has been long lost. Now the Faerie Carbuncle is nothing more than a very rare and expensive bit of jewelry which has been part of the museum collection for several hundred years."

"Quite right," said Mr. Glump, who now stood at the inspector's side. "That is a remarkably smart bird you have, Miss Crate. But unfortunately, as I believe I have told you before, there are no pets allowed in the museum. Now, off with you both."

The inspector and the curator walked back to Elbert Hackelsmith, the night watchman.

"Pet?" Deacon nearly shouted. "I never."

Oona shushed him before whispering: "I have an idea."

"An idea? For what?"

Oona did not answer, but instead bid the daytime museum guard good-bye and made as if she were heading toward the staircase to the library. Glancing over her shoulder, she saw that the guard had turned his attention back toward the center of the room. Oona quickly jumped behind one of the enormous rectangular stones.

"What are you doing?" Deacon asked.

"Getting closer so I can listen," Oona said, as if it should be obvious.

"We don't have time for this."

"Shush."

Like a pouncing cat she leapt the open distance to the next stone. She paused a moment with her back against the stone, waiting for someone to come looking. No one came.

The conversation between the night watchman and the inspector was louder now, but she needed to get closer still if she wanted to hear everything that was being said.

"I need to get closer."

"Have you completely lost your mind?"

"Just one more stone," she said, and poked her head around the corner. There was a problem. If she crossed now, she would be in clear view of the daytime guard. She pulled back behind the stone and bit her lip, thinking. "I need a distraction, Deacon."

"Don't look at me," he said. "I'm supposed to be gone, along with you."

"That's true," Oona said, and then, realizing she had no alternative, she pulled her magnifying glass from her dress pocket and gripped it tightly at her side. Peering around the corner of the stone, her gaze fell upon a portrait on the other side of the room: a rather hairy-looking goblin wearing a wooden crown. With his saggy green skin and large fanged teeth, the goblin king looked old and feeble, not to mention quite angry that he had been forced to sit so long for the portrait.

Oona raised her magnifying glass and took aim at the portrait. "*Aldis-tractio.*"

A wisp of misty light shot from the end of the magnifying glass and struck the portrait between the eyes. The goblin began to blink his eyes rapidly before letting out a horrific sneeze.

The museum guard turned and began to walk in the direction of the sound as Oona bolted across the open space between the stones and came to a sliding stop. Deacon joined her as she peered around the corner to discover the day guard standing in front of the goblin portrait, his brow furrowed in confusion.

"Let's go over it one more time," Inspector White said.

"I've already told you twice," came a voice that Oona assumed to be the night watchman's.

"Perhaps you are forgetting something," Mr. Glump said.

"I'm not forgetting anything!" the inspector snapped.

"No, Inspector, I was speaking to Mr. Hackelsmith."

"Of course," the inspector said. "I knew that. I was just testing you."

Oona placed a hand over her eyes and shook her head. She still could not believe that this buffoon was the head of the Dark Street Police Department.

"So, it was nine o'clock last night when I stepped out the front door for some fresh air and to eat my apple, see?" Night Watchman Hackelsmith began. "Nothing out of the ordinary. I always have an apple around nine o'clock out on the steps, but last night was different. See, last night, I'd just taken a bite when a woman comes running up the steps waving her arms and all out of breath like, right? I can hear her saying something about needing help, but it's all under her breath."

"Did you get a look at her face?" the inspector asked.

"No," Hackelsmith said. "Her face was all in shadow on account of the great big hat she was wearing, and all the streetlights were behind her, so she was...what's that called, when the light is behind and their front is too dark to see?"

"Silhouetted," Deacon whispered in Oona's ear, and Oona grinned. One of the many books stored in Deacon's brain was the *Oxford English Dictionary*, which, along with the *Dark Street Who's Who*—a book that briefly described the lives of nearly every inhabitant on the street—came in quite handy. Thinking of the *Who's Who*, Oona made a mental note to ask Deacon about Mr. Hackelsmith.

"You mean the woman was *silhouetted*?" asked Mr. Glump.

"Yeah, that's it," the night watchman continued. "I couldn't see her face. But when I moved forward to see what was the matter, something hit me on the back of my head and I just sort of...well, it all went black."

"And how long were you out?" the inspector asked.

"Not sure. Next thing I know, I'm all tied up, and my head is fit to burst. Takes me a minute to realize that I'm lying right here, in the middle of the entryway, and I hear voices."

"What did the voices say?"

"Well, it was hard to understand them, 'cause there's a terrible ringing in my ears, see? Everything had a strange echo, but the first voice was definitely a woman's. That I'm sure of."

"The same woman you heard on the steps?" The inspector asked.

"Possibly," Hackelsmith said. "Like I said, my ears were ringing. Anyway, she says: 'We've got it. Let's get out of here.' And then comes a man's voice. He was harder to understand, 'cause of my pulsing head, but I'm pretty sure he says: 'Shush, he'll hear you.' Then the front door slams, and I'm forced to lie there all night until Victor finds me and cuts me free in the morning."

"Victor is the daytime guard?" Inspector White asked.

"Yeah, that's me," came the deep voice of the day guard. But to Oona's surprise, she realized the voice was not coming from the other side of the room, but from right behind her.

She jumped as she spun around to find the thickset guard staring down at her, arms crossed, fingers drumming his forearms. She winced, rebuking herself inwardly for getting so lost in the conversation that she had failed to notice the guard sneak up on her.

"Look at what I found here," the guard said, and grabbed her by the arm. Deacon cawed threateningly at the big man, and the guard jerked back from the bird's fluttering wings, but he did not let go.

"What is the meaning of this?" Inspector White demanded as Oona was forcefully pulled from her hiding place and shoved into the circle of stones.

She stumbled into the center, where her foot seemed to get tangled in something and she fell to the floor. She was not hurt, though the shock of the fall startled her. She looked quickly at her feet to find what had caused her fall. It was the rope that had been used to tie up the night watchman.

"I...I can explain," she stammered, and reached for the rope to untangle her feet.

The inspector's nostrils flared. "You can explain yourself right into a police dungeon, Miss Crate!"

"Inspector, I was only trying to—" But her words stopped abruptly as her eyes came to rest on the knot that had been used on the rope. Her eyes went wide with astonishment, and her mouth went dry.

"No more excuses, Miss Crate!" the inspector shouted at her. "I have told you for the last time..."

But Oona was hardly listening. Every bit of her consciousness was focused on the peculiar knot that had been used to tie up the night watchman. It was an extraordinary knot. Beautiful, in fact. It looked like a rose.

She pulled it closer, running her thumb over its petal-like complexity, marveling at its perfection. Indeed, she might have said that she had never seen anything like it...and yet she *had* seen it before, not in real life, but as a sketch in an old police report—a report that Oona had read countless times over the past three years. It was a famous knot in the world of criminals, and there were only two people whom Oona knew for sure were capable of tying it.

She pushed herself to her feet and held the knotted rope in front of her, surprised that Inspector White had not recognized it straightaway—but then again, Inspector White probably did not study old case files. Currently, the inspector was rambling on about putting her in a jail cell for her own good.

"Hey, look at what she's got there," said one of the police constables.

The inspector gave the man a nasty look for

interrupting him, but then another of the constables put in: "Oh. How could we have missed that?"

"Missed what?" the inspector said incredulously.

"The Rose Knot," said the first constable.

The inspector cast several confused looks at his constables before stating: "Ah...of course. The Rose Knot."

It was clear to Oona that the inspector did not understand the significance.

"The only two people known to tie a knot like this," Oona said, "are the infamous Rose Thieves. This is their signature."

The second constable scratched thoughtfully at his balding head. "But the Rose Thieves have not struck for years."

Oona's heart felt as if it were making its way up into her throat. "Not for over three years. They disappeared from the criminal world the very day that they...killed my father." Her voice shook slightly, and her fingers gripped the rope in a pale fist. The sudden burst of emotion threatened to explode.

Deacon shivered on her shoulder. "It would seem they have returned."

Chapter Three

The Critic

Oona quickly ascended the stairs that rose along the side wall of the museum entryway to the library. Deacon clung precariously to her shoulder as she bounded up the steps, her mind racing. And yet it was difficult for her to follow any one thought before a sting of anger would obliterate it completely.

The knowledge that her father's killers had never been brought to justice had angered her for years.

"You know, you are lucky that the inspector let you go," Deacon said. "I thought for sure he was going to arrest you this time."

"Is that all you have to say?" Oona snapped at him, and then immediately felt guilty for it. "What more can you tell me of the Faerie Carbuncle, Deacon; this magical gemstone that was stolen?"

"There is not much to tell," Deacon said. "It is more of a legend than anything else. The magical powers it is purported to have given to its wearers are only accessed by a spell that has been long forgotten. Perhaps there is a mention of it in more obscure magical texts, but as you know, the

Encyclopedia Arcanna is mostly an historical reference and has no mention of actual spell work. I can tell you, however, that as far as anyone actually receiving faerielike powers from the stone, it has not happened in over six hundred years. That's over a hundred years before Oswald the Great closed the Glass Gates. Some historians believe that the written spell was lost in Faerie, and has since been forgotten."

"Should we then assume that the thieves stole it simply for its value as a gemstone?" Oona asked.

"Unless the thieves know something that historians don't," Deacon said, "it is probably safe to assume."

Oona let out a heavy breath as they reached the top landing. She did not like the fact that the thieves had stolen such a potentially powerful object, despite the lost spell.

"But for the moment," Deacon added, "there is nothing we can do about it, and I really think you should return to the Pendulum House library and learn all you can about this battle test."

Oona experienced a twisting sensation in the pit of her stomach. She knew Deacon was right, and yet still she felt compelled to pursue the investigation first and foremost.

She pushed through the library door. "There will be time to research the battle test later. But first we need to do a little research here, in the *public* library."

"But I've told you, the best books on magic reside at Pendulum House."

Oona shook her head. "It's not books on magic I'm looking for."

"Then what?"

Oona sighed, as if the answer should be self-evident. "We need to find books on knots. Now, where to begin?"

She peered around the enormous room, unsure of where to start. As the outside of the building suggested, the new library was cone shaped on the inside, with level upon level of rising balconies that supported countless shelves of books. Unlike the Pendulum House library, the books here appeared to be shelved in an expertly ordered fashion. The bottom floor consisted of various chairs and tables topped with dim reading lights.

Oona approached the reference desk. Her face grew warm as the boy behind the counter looked up from his book cart and grinned. The odd assortment of symbols tattooed on his cheeks and around his eyes pulled tight.

"Ah, hello, Miss Crate," said Adler Iree in his lilting Irish brogue. "Fancy meeting you here."

Oona smiled back. Despite having told him many times to call her Oona—not to mention the fact that he had kissed her at Oswald Park...on the lips—he still insisted upon calling her Miss Crate. She wondered if it was his way of telling her that the kiss had not meant all that much. After all, it had been four whole months since that first kiss, and she had not received a second.

Of course, Adler had been extremely busy with his studies at the Magicians Legal Alliance—the guild and school for the practitioners of magical law. He was taking a full course load, and on top of that—as part of the alliance's community outreach program—he was now volunteering at the library as a part-time "book-shelving expert." With Oona's own apprentice duties, the two of them had had little time to see each other over the past months, and when they did, they were never alone.

But still, she had hoped that he would ask her to be his girlfriend. Many girls Oona's age had steady boyfriends— such as Adler's own sister Isadora Iree, who took every opportunity to remind people who her handsome boyfriend was—and Oona was beginning to wonder if Adler was simply against the idea.

"Hello, Adler," she said, hoping he would pick up on her use of his first name.

He moved closer to the desk and squinted at her. "Everything all right?"

She tucked her hair behind her ear. "Yes...I mean, no. I

mean..." And she told him all about the crime scene downstairs and the connection with her father.

He tilted his top hat back and leaned on the desk. "And no one knows who the Rose Thieves are?"

"Not a clue," Oona said. "I've looked through my father's personal file on them countless times, and there are no names. Just that they were known associates of Red Martin. But of course, I've known they were working for him ever since Red Martin admitted to me that he was the one who paid to have my father murdered. The Rose Thieves staged a robbery, and when my father showed up to apprehend them, they shot him dead and then tied a ribbon in the shape of a rose around the gun and left it at the scene of the crime. That was their signature. They would break into a rich household, steal a prized possession like a painting or jewelry, and leave behind a bit of ribbon tied like a rose."

Adler frowned. "How do you know the robbery that your father was investigating was staged?"

"Two reasons. The thieves were perfectionists, brilliant and arrogant, leaving behind their signature knot wherever they struck. It was one of the reasons my father wanted to catch them so badly. They were never seen coming or going from the crime scene. But the police received a tip that someone saw two masked figures crawling in through a second-story window in broad daylight. The supposed thieves made sure they were seen. My father must have thought it was just an ordinary burglary. And the second reason I know the robbery was a setup is because the apartment was vacant. There was no one living there and nothing to steal. The thieves made sure they were seen breaking in, and then waited there. They shot both my father and the constable he had with him the instant they came through the door, and then left the gun with the ribbon tied to it in the center of the empty room. Many people heard the shots, but no one saw the murderers flee."

Deacon put in: "And there have been no Rose Knots

left on the street since."

"Not until today," Oona said.

Adler walked around the desk, scratching absently at his cheek, where Oona just now realized he had a fresh symbol tattooed. This one looked a bit like a squiggle set inside of a triangle, and she realized that he must have completed a new course of study at the alliance. Many of the alliance's older members had completed so many courses that their faces were completely covered in multicolored tattoos. She hoped Adler did not become so ambitious.

"So I need to find books about knot tying," she said.

Adler nodded understandingly. "To see if you can't find some clue about that Rose Knot that leads you to the thieves?"

Oona nodded, excited that they were following the same train of thought. "I had never seen the actual knot until today, except as an illustration, but I'll bet we can find something about it in a book that—"

Deacon cleared his throat.

Oona sighed. "Ah, but as Deacon keeps reminding me, I do have other obligations today."

"And don't you have obligations as well, Mr. Iree?" a new voice interrupted. "Such as putting away books?"

The voice was bright, and girlish, and sweet. They turned to find a young woman of about eighteen years old watching them from behind the reference desk. Her pretty, slender face was framed by straight red hair that parted down the middle and fell freely down her shoulders.

Adler cleared his throat and turned to Oona. "Ah, Miss Crate, may I introduce you to Miss Mary Shusher, the assistant librarian."

Oona smiled graciously. "How do you do?"

Mary Shusher raised both eyebrows in surprise. "You didn't tell me you knew the Wizard's apprentice, Adler." She extended her hand to Oona, and they shook. "I've read all about you. In the paper. About your exploits. You're the one who finally completed the Magician's Tower."

Oona's face flushed. The fact that she was a celebrity on the street was something she had never gotten used to.

"So, is it true?" Mary asked before Oona could respond. "Are you a genuine Natural Magician?" Oona opened her mouth to reply, but Mary did not wait for an answer. "That's incredibly rare. Only one born in every hundred years, or something like that. It is said that you have the same natural abilities as a faerie, and that you can do all sorts of magic without having to study."

Deacon responded before Oona could open her mouth. "While Learned Magicians, such as the Wizard, must study for decades to learn their craft, a Natural Magician, such as Miss Crate, has active faerie blood in her veins. Like a faerie, Natural Magicians are born with incredible magical abilities. But *unlike* a faerie, they are not born with the instincts to control the magic they possess. They must be trained."

Mary Shusher leaned eagerly over the counter and asked: "Can we see some magic."

Oona hesitated. Magic was not something that she took lightly. Despite her extraordinary powers, she rarely used a spell if there was an alternative, and using magic to impress someone was the last thing she wished to do. After all, that was precisely what she had been doing three years ago—trying to impress her mother—when she had cast *Lux lucis admiratio.*

One moment she had been a happy ten-year-old wielding her makeshift magic wand (a fallen twig she'd found in the park) and watching the Lights of Wonder light up the sky, and the next instant the spell was flying violently out of control. The lights crashed into the great fig tree with such force that it simultaneously burst into flames and crashed to the ground, crushing her mother and baby sister beneath its massive trunk and changing Oona's life forever.

All of that from one spell, a complex and powerful spell, yes, but it was a stark reminder that magic such as she possessed was not to be taken lightly. Causing a distraction in the museum entryway was one thing—at least then she was trying to accomplish something important, like eavesdropping on an investigation. But doing magic for no good reason...or to show off...she was soundly against it.

Seeming to read Oona's reticence, Mary Shusher said sweetly: "Oh, please. Just something small, like levitating this book." She eagerly placed a reference book on the counter, a clothbound volume entitled *Butterflies of the World.* "Just flip its pages open or something, without touching it."

Oona looked from the book to Adler. He grinned.

"Only if you want to," he said, though she could tell by the way his eyes widened that he was eager to see her perform. She recalled that he had only seen her do magic twice before, and that both times he had been quite impressed.

She considered the book for a moment.

It would not be hard to do, flip it open, even levitate it from across the room. It was a simple enough conductor spell that required nothing more than a wand—or, in Oona's case, her magnifying glass—to focus and aim the energy.

She removed the magnifying glass from her pocket—her father's gold-rimmed magnifying glass, her dearest possession in the world—and aimed it at the book.

"Alum," she said.

The book rose several inches off the countertop and flipped open. It spun around on a cushion of air, as if turned by unseen fingers. It was an easy spell, one her uncle encouraged her to use, and one that he himself used to levitate teacups and glasses during his many parties at Pendulum House.

The thought of her uncle reminded her of the battle test she was supposed to be preparing for. Something much more demanding was waiting for her at three o'clock, she was pretty sure of that, and the thought caused her

—

concentration to waiver. The book tumbled in the air, as if the invisible fingers had gone suddenly clumsy. She tightened her grip on the magnifying glass, meaning to refocus her energy, but the book thumped back to the countertop with a crack that echoed around the library.

Adler grinned ear to ear. "That was most excellent, so it was!"

Even Deacon—who had seen her do much more complicated spells, but was always keen on her use of magic—flapped his wings excitedly. "Bravo!"

But when Oona looked to Mary Shusher, the assistant librarian's mouth turned to a frown. She seemed to be pleased and unpleased at the same moment.

"Well, it started out all right," Mary said encouragingly. "The spinning about was a nice touch, but then it got all wibbly-wobbly. It seemed to me as if your heart was just not in it."

Oona blinked several times in surprise. "My...my heart?"

"That's when the entire spell simply failed," Mary continued sweetly. "You might consider letting the book ease back down slowly next time, for a more refined finish. All in all, I give it three and a half stars."

Oona's mouth fell open as she stared at the assistant librarian.

"That's out of five," Mary said earnestly.

"Three and a half?" Oona said indignantly, and then, realizing what the young woman was doing, she added: "Are you critiquing my spell work? Rating it with stars?"

Mary smiled brightly. "I came up with that system myself."

Adler gestured toward Mary. "Oh, I probably should have told you. Mary is training to be a critic."

"I prefer the term 'reviewer,'" Mary said, and then, seeing the pinched expression on Oona's face, she added: "I hope I haven't offended you. Please don't take it personally. I

---

was only trying to be helpful."

And from her tone, Oona could tell that the young lady was indeed trying to be helpful. Yet despite Mary's intentions, not to mention the fact that she had been correct that Oona had been distracted, Oona still could not help but want to tell Mary to mind her own business. She doubted that Mary had ever even attempted a spell, let alone floated a book off a table.

Sensing Oona's building tension, Deacon said: "The art of the critique has been around for as long as there has been art to criticize, even in the earliest civilizations. A well-respected critic not only acts as a discerning voice for the general public, helping them make informed decisions on how to spend their time and money, but also as constructive feedback to the artists so they can grow in their craft."

Oona continued to frown. "But in the end, it's still just one person's opinion."

"True," Deacon said. "But a respected and well informed opinion. The critic is an authority on the subject they are discussing. At least that is the general idea."

Oona scratched at her head, wondering if Mary considered herself to be an authority on the subject of magic.

Mary sighed, her bright eyes all at once downcast, and Oona wondered if she had hurt the young woman's feelings.

"I'm afraid that my mother shares your view," Mary said softly. "She wishes for me to become a full-fledged librarian like her. And please don't misunderstand me, I do love the library. My mother has a very important job. It's just that...well, I want to review more than just books. There are all sorts of things to critique. Food. Clothing. Theater. I'd like to have my very own column in the *Dark Street Tribune*. I would be the first woman to do so, you know. That would be something, wouldn't it? And everyone will read it, and…" Again she sighed. "And...well, it's a dream of mine."

She looked suddenly sad, and Oona felt a twang of guilt as she realized that Mary Shusher and she had something in common: they both felt pressure to follow in family occupations, and yet they both had other aspirations.

Oona was on the verge of telling Mary about her own dream of becoming a full-time detective, despite the pressure to become the next Wizard, when the thought reminded her of her mission. She was on a case, and it occurred to her that Mary Shusher could quite possibly be a suspect in the museum theft. Indeed, everyone who worked at the library or regularly used the museum entrance should be considered a person of interest.

"Tell me, Mary, where were you last night at nine o'clock?"

Mary was clearly surprised by the abrupt change of subject. Her well-manicured fingers began to play nervously with her hair. "I...I was at home, with my grandmother."

Oona eyed the assistant librarian carefully. She could not say why, but she had a feeling Mary was not being completely truthful. Before, when Mary had been critiquing Oona's spell work, there had been an earnestness about her words, a self-assuredness, and yet now she seemed to hesitate.

Oona decided to press further. "Do you live with your grandmother?"

Mary's eyes shifted about. "She lives with us, yes."

"Us?"

"With my parents and me. What is this about?"

Oona continued to watch her closely. "Are you aware that the museum was broken into last night? That a valuable object was stolen?"

Mary nodded. "I know that the night watchman was attacked. We were told as much this morning when we came to work. I did not know anything was stolen."

"We?" Oona asked.

"My mother and me. Why are you so interested in—"
But Mary was cut short when a hidden door behind the desk opened and a bespectacled woman with dazzlingly large

green eyes stepped through the doorway. Her red hair was cut unfashionably short, stopping just below her ears, and the hair was oddly stiff. It did not seem to move at all as she walked, and it reminded Oona of a metal helmet.

Aside from her hair, however, the woman's own movements were smooth and quick, almost catlike, as she approached the counter. Similar to the lab coats that were the new fashion for doctors, she wore a long black jacket that covered her from neck to ankle and had pockets in the front. Her powdered face stood out in stark contrast, and was an older version of Mary's, her eyes highly alert.

She smiled.

"Who is making all of that noise with their mouths?" she asked in a soft whisper. Surprisingly, she did not sound upset...and yet Oona could not help but feel nervous. There was an edge to the woman's presence, a sharpness. Here was a woman whose authority required no raising of voice or disapproving stares.

"Oh, sorry, Mother," Mary replied respectfully.

"Volume," the older Mrs. Shusher said, her voice even quieter than before. "Voices down. This is a library, not an opera house." Her eyes went from Adler to Mary. As her gaze fell on her daughter, she sighed. "And back to work, both of you. Those books aren't going to shelve themselves."

Hardly sparing a glance at Oona, Mrs. Shusher turned back to the hidden door. For a moment Oona could only watch her, captivated not only by her unique sense of style but also her manner. But then she remembered her mission. Oona moved forward, hoping to ask the librarian about her whereabouts the previous night. Mary seized Oona's hand and shook her head. A moment later the librarian had closed the hidden door and was gone.

Oona pulled her hand from Mary's and flexed her fingers. "What was that about?"

"You must keep your voice down," Mary said seriously. "My mother is in a foul temper these days, ever since I told her of my dream to become a reviewer...and if you push her with your questions, I'm afraid she'll kick you out of the library." She hesitated for a moment before adding: "And besides, my birthday is at the end of the week, and I'm afraid if I irritate her even more then I won't get the present I asked for."

Oona scowled but managed to keep her voice at a whisper. "All I was going to ask was—"

"Was where she was at around nine o'clock last night, yes?" Mary said. "Well, I can tell you that. Last night was Monday night, and my mother and father have a literary club they attend every Monday, Wednesday, and Friday from eight until ten o'clock at the Stratford Learning Center."

Oona raised an eyebrow. "That's a lot of nights for a literary club."

Mary shrugged. "They love books."

Deacon shifted excitedly from one foot to the other. "Sounds wonderful."

Mary picked the butterfly book up off the counter and placed it on the shelf behind her.

"And what is the present you asked for?" Oona asked.

Mary considered the question for several seconds. "I'd rather not say just now," she said before leaning over the counter, her voice dropping into an even quieter whisper. "I don't want to jinx it." She nodded conspiratorially toward the hidden door and then stood up straight. "Anyway, my mother is right, Adler. We need to return to work."

And with that Mary Shusher rounded the counter and strode across the library toward the stairs to the second level.

Oona stared after her, shaking her head at the ridiculous excuse Mary had given for keeping her wish a secret.

Doesn't want to jinx it? she thought. *What an absurd idea. Talking about something doesn't jinx anything.*

"What say we find some books on knots, eh?" Adler said in a hushed tone. "The library is divided into categories by subject, so I'd suggest we look under books on sailing. There's bound to be some books on knots there."

Oona heaved a sigh before agreeing to search for books about sailing. As they looked, Oona couldn't help but wonder what the present was that Mary was expecting from her parents, and why she wouldn't just tell Oona what it was.

"Here're the three books on sailing knots I could find," Adler said, handing three thin books to Oona. They placed them on one of the reference tables and went through page by page. Each contained illustrations showing how to tie various sailors' knots crucial to life on a sailboat. Oona thought fondly of how her mother, who had been a lover of all things having to do with boats, would have enjoyed reading through these pages with her.

But as much as Oona marveled over the various knots, none of them came close to the level of sophistication used by the thieves. The knots in these books were useful, but none as stunningly beautiful as that of the Rose Knot.

Undaunted, Adler suggested they next search under the subject of construction.

"Builders need to use knots all the time on construction sites," he said.

Again Oona thought this was an excellent suggestion. As they perused the shelves, Oona stole several glances at Adler.

This section of the library was on the third floor and quite abandoned. The thought of the kiss he had given her all those months ago drifted across her memory like a leaf floating on a spring breeze. She glanced nervously around. Now would be an opportune moment to make such a magical moment happen again...if he chose to.

He seemed to sense her gaze. He turned to her, and their eyes met. He did not move. An outrageous thought sprang into Oona's mind—one that made all the tiny nerves tingle along her arms.

I could be the one to kiss him.

But the thought made her too nervous, and she shoved it aside the best she could. Silence. Deacon cleared his throat rather loudly from his perch on a nearby shelf, and Oona jumped. She had forgotten Deacon was there, and both she and Adler hurriedly returned their attention to the shelves.

"I was thinking," she said offhandedly, though in truth her stomach felt as if she had swallowed a swarm of frantic butterflies, "that perhaps you would like to accompany me to the campaign rally for Molly Morgana Moon on Thursday."

"Thursday?" Adler said thoughtfully. He continued to run his fingers along the book spines. "I have a test at the Magicians Alliance that day"

"Oh, I see," Oona said, unable to conceal her disappointment.

Adler cocked an eyebrow. "But the test is in the morning. I should be done by noontime. Isn't the rally planned for one o'clock?"

Oona's spirits lifted. "At Oswald Park. You already know about it?"

He nodded. "My mother and sister are already planning on going. They're big Molly Morgana Moon supporters...so perhaps I'll tag along?" He returned his attention to the bookshelves before adding: "I could meet you there."

Oona swallowed a rather large lump in her throat. "Very good."

It turned out there were even fewer books on construction knots than on sailing knots. Indeed, they found only one, and it contained mostly illustrations of the same sort of knots they had found in the sailing books.

"Hmm," Oona said as she slid the book back into place on the shelf. "This seems to be getting us nowhere."

"Speaking of getting us nowhere," Deacon said, "the time for your test is getting close, and we have done no preparation or research." He flew to the nearby balcony and peered down toward the large clock on the main floor. "You have only an hour to get ready."

"An hour?" Oona said sharply. "Deacon, how come you didn't remind me earlier?"

"Oh, it's my fault now, is it?" Deacon asked.

"What sort of test?" Adler asked.

But Oona was already moving toward the stairs. "I'll tell you later. I have to run. Thank you, Adler."

"Any time, Oona," Adler replied with a quick tip of the hat.

It wasn't until she was outside and stepping up into the carriage that she realized he had used her first name.

Chapter Four

The First Test

"The test you are about to experience is not one of my design," the Wizard said. He pushed back his seat and made as if to stand, but his long beard, which trailed down his chest as twisted and gray as a summer tornado, snagged on one of the hooked claws that poked out from the desk, and he was suddenly jerked forward.

"Oh, are you okay, Uncle?" Oona asked. She stepped hurriedly around the desk to help him.

He waived her back. "It's all right. This has happened before. Now, where's my wand?"

Oona had to stifle a laugh. It was a comical sight, seeing her uncle, the prestigious Wizard of Dark Street, bent forward over the ominous dragon-bone desk with his beard caught on the claw like a fish on a hook.

"Ah, here it is," he said, removing his wand from his pocket and aiming it at the bottom of his beard. "Trim," he said.

The distinctive sound of metal scissors cutting through hair reached Oona's ears in the same instant that the Wizard stood upright, his beard decidedly less pointy than it had been.

"I've been meaning to have a trim anyway," he said, fingering the flat spot at the bottom of his beard, and when he looked at Oona and saw her attempting to hide her smile, his face reddened considerably.

"You were saying, Uncle?" Oona said, only just managing to keep from giggling.

"Saying?" said the Wizard.

"About the test," said Deacon, who was not as successful at holding back his laughter as Oona.

The Wizard picked the severed end of his beard from the claw on the desk and tossed it to the floor. "Yes, the test. As I was saying. It is a test that all apprentices must undergo when they are ready. One that I faced when I was an apprentice myself, long before I became a comical old man." He gave Deacon a shrewd look, and Deacon's laughter came to an abrupt halt.

"Of course, sir," Deacon said, with a clearing of his throat.

Uncle Alexander returned his gaze to Oona as he moved out from behind the desk. "The test is quite difficult, but I think you will manage, Oona dear. Especially if you were able to prepare yourself."

The Wizard gave her a shrewd look, as if he somehow knew that Oona had not given herself sufficient time to find anything in the Pendulum House library on the tests. Such information would likely have been quite easy to find, had Samuligan been around to find the book she needed, but the moment they had returned to the house, the faerie servant had disappeared, and no matter how many times Oona had called for him, he had not shown up.

This was unlike Samuligan, who was usually no more than a few feet away after she called for him in the house. She needed only to shout his name and he would appear from out of a shadow, or from behind a drapery, or on the other side of the nearest door. No such luck today.

Without the faerie's help, Oona found the organization of the library to be nonexistent. If only, like the public library, the books had been organized into subjects, and authors, and alphabetical titles.

Deacon cawed from his place on the fireplace mantel, sounding his disapproval of how she had handled her time. She threw a hard glance his way as Uncle Alexander moved around the slumbering dragon-bone desk and peered at the clock. The hour hand struck three o'clock, and he began to nod.

"As you know, Oona, when you become Wizard, it will be your job to protect Dark Street and the World of Man beyond."

"World of Humans," Oona interrupted.

The Wizard nodded, but absently, as if he had not truly heard her. "Should the Glass Gates fall, you alone must hold back the wrath of the faerie queen, her army of faerie warriors, and all the might of the Other-lands. The question that every apprentice eventually asks is: How can one person accomplish such a seemingly daunting task? And the answer stands all around you: Pendulum House. The Magicians of Old pooled all of their powers into the house long ago, and the Wizard's job is to tap into that power and direct it to do his or her will. And that is what we will be training and testing you on today: your ability to link with the house."

Oona's heart began to beat a little faster. She had never tapped into the house's powers before. She had always used her own Natural Magic. She was often aware of the immense power that was locked inside of the house as she walked down its unpredictable hallways, or as she lay in bed at night—sensing that the house easily dwarfed her own extraordinary natural powers—and it frightened her a bit to consider how she might control such a force.

The Wizard ran his fingers down his beard. "Your task shall be to feed off the house's magic, and use that power to overcome and defeat your opponent."

"My opponent?" Oona asked.

Again the Wizard continued on as if he had not heard her. "Since it is your first time linking with the house, we

—

44

will set you a simple task...simple in the sense that you have only one clear objective...but remarkably difficult in all other aspects. Once you *tap in*, your job will be to reach the Pendulum House front gates by whatever means necessary."

Oona furrowed her brow, thinking she had not heard correctly. "Did you say all I need to do is walk out to the front gates?"

The Wizard grinned. It was a knowing sort of smile, one that assured her there was something much more complex happening. Yet what could be so complex about walking from the Wizard's study to the front gates? It was nearly a straight line out the study door, across the circular antechamber, past the broom closet in the entryway, and out through the front door. From there the course involved a bit of bobbing and weaving through the tangled vegetation of the front garden to an old iron gate that opened upon Dark Street, but Oona managed that time and again each day.

"I said nothing about walking," the Wizard replied rather cryptically. "I merely stated that you would need to get there by whatever means necessary."

Oona looked to Deacon on the mantel, but he only cocked his head to one side and said nothing. He did not need to say a word. She could hear his voice in her head loud and clear: *You should have spent your time researching the test.*

Oona reminded herself that this was not just a test, but a *battle test*—whatever that meant.

Her uncle read her expression and nodded, his wrinkled hand continuing to run down his beard, which fluttered in the rising warmth of the nearby fire. He seemed to be waiting for her to speak.

"My...opponent," she said hesitantly. "My opponent will try to stop me from getting there."

The Wizard clapped his hands together, causing the fire in the fireplace to briefly burn blue. "That is precisely right. Might I introduce you to him? Samuligan!" he called.

Samuligan leapt from the shadow of the grandfather

clock, his hooked nose and long faerie face shadowed beneath his cowboy hat. He landed in front of the door with a resounding *clang*, the sound emanating from the black body armor he was wearing. Coupled with the cowboy hat, Oona thought the faerie servant looked quite comical, as if he were going to a costume party and could not decide what he wanted to be.

She nearly laughed until it occurred to her that Samuligan was not here to *fetch* her opponent, but that he *was* her opponent. The comical effect quickly disappeared when she noticed streaks of dried blood speckled across the dark dented metal, and more dried rivulets of blood that had never been properly cleaned from the various spikes and rivets at the shoulder and elbow joints.

The armor had a kind of negative glow about it, she noticed, a sinister presence that seemed to suck all the light off its surface rather than reflect it; and yet Oona could see the story that the blood told quite well. This armor was battle tested, and battle proven...and she—a four-foot-five-inch-tall, thirteen-year-old girl—most certainly was not. She had a strange feeling that the armor itself wanted to bite her and chew her up. It was faerie-made armor, she realized, and just to look at it made her insides feel as if they had all shriveled up.

She swallowed dryly, remembering how nearly five hundred years ago, Samuligan the Fay had been a powerful general in the Queen of Faerie's royal army during the Great Faerie War. Looking at him now, in his daunting attire, she could see why even Oswald the Great had feared him; and why, when the faerie had been captured, the Magicians of Old had used their magic to trap Samuligan into a life of servitude to the members of Pendulum House.

"But surely Samuligan is not allowed to harm me," Oona said, and she could hear the nervousness in her own voice.

Samuligan seemed to hear it, too. He grinned his

horrible grin. His eyes sparkled with a kind of otherworldly delight beneath the brim of his hat, and though she loved the faerie servant very much, and trusted him with her very life, she shivered to have that look directed at her.

"He will not harm you," the Wizard tried to assure her, but Samuligan's crescent moon of a smile suggested otherwise. "He's just excited because he only gets to do this every new generation. No, he will not hurt you—not on purpose, that is—but what he will do is attempt to stop you from achieving your goal, from reaching the front gate. And he is very good at it, I can assure you. He tested me, and Armand Flirtensnickle before me, and all the apprentices going back for hundreds of years. He has always done so, for who better than an actual battle-hardened faerie to prepare an apprentice for battle against faeries?"

Oona briefly wondered if Samuligan might take offense at the Wizard's eagerness to defeat faeries in battle. But if Samuligan did take offense, he never showed it, and indeed, looking at him now, he seemed quite eager to start Oona's training to do just that.

"But first," said the Wizard, and he held up a finger to make his point. "First you must tap into the source of every presiding Wizard's magic. You must link with the house. I think you will need this,"

He pulled from his pocket a slim black wand and handed it to Oona. It was not the Wizard's own wand, for her uncle's wand was brown and made of ornately carved oak. This wand was smooth, and glossy, and black as night. It was a wand that Oona had held before, months ago, when she had removed it from the black box at the top of the Magician's Tower. It was Oswald the Great's very own wand.

It felt cold in her hand, like cool metal, though she knew it to be made of wood. Such great things this wand had done, remarkable feats that now resided in the history books. From her history lessons with Deacon she could name half a dozen off the top of her head, not the least of which included the permanent closing of the Glass Gates. It was said that this wand was the only key to opening those gates.

It made her nervous just to hold it. Ever since her discovery of the wand, it had resided within its protective box and been hidden safely away within the house, its location known only to the Wizard.

"You are no doubt wondering why I have given you Oswald's wand," the Wizard said.

Oona considered him for only the briefest of moments before answering: "A link with the house must require a conductor. A wand or staff. But I already have my magnifying glass, which has proven just as competent as any wand."

In fact, the Wizard had offered to make a wand for her—a "proper wand" had been his precise words—but Oona had declined. She preferred the smooth wood handle and glossy golden ring of her magnifying glass, which held much more meaning for her than any silly bit of wood. It had been her father's magnifying glass, and though he had not been a magician himself, Oona always felt a part of him was with her, guiding her, when she held it in her hand.

The thought reminded her of the very people who had been responsible for his death, and that they were out there now, back at their nefarious deeds.

"Actually, a link with the house does not require a conductor," the Wizard said. "But once you have achieved the initial link, and you wish to use that power to achieve some task or another, a wand is then most advisable. The power you are connecting with is like that of nothing you have ever experienced before, Oona. I fear that your magnifying glass, as fine as it is for everyday spell work, may not be up to the task. I could not guarantee its safety, and I know how much you cherish it. You would not want it ruined."

Oona nodded thoughtfully, her nerves doubling up inside of her.

"Oswald's wand," the Wizard continued, "is perfectly suited for this task. Now, are you ready to link with the house?"

Oona shook her head no, but what came out of her mouth was: "I suppose."

Uncle Alexander smiled reassuringly. "Come now, don't look so frightened. As I said, Samuligan will not hurt you."

She let out a quick *tsk* sound, not because she disbelieved her uncle, but because it wasn't Samuligan she was afraid of. Well, *mostly* it wasn't Samuligan. Rather, it was the magic she was about to connect with that she feared. She had experienced great power before, her own, and had thought that magic barely controllable. Though she did feel somewhat comforted with the fact that both her uncle and Samuligan would be here if anything went too wrong...she hoped.

"Now, what I want you to do is stand here, beside the desk, and face Samuligan. Once you link with the house, he is going to do everything he can to keep you from leaving the room."

Oona took her place beside the slowly breathing desk, glancing at Deacon as she did so. He was shifting nervously from one foot to the other. Samuligan stood directly in front of her, his menacing armor clinking as he, too, shifted from side to side.

"May the best man win," the faerie said.

"But you are not a man, and neither am I," she said.

"Lucky for us," he said, his eyes flashing wide. "I'm pretty sure a man could not do this."

The faerie tilted his head back and pulled a three-foot broad sword from his mouth.

Deacon tutted from the mantel. "A carnival man's trick."

Samuligan raised an eyebrow at the raven. "Ah, but could a carnival man do this, as well?"

And to everyone's astonishment, he raised a gauntleted hand to his mouth and withdrew an entire wooden shield, the edges stretching his grin bizarrely as it slid from the cavern of his mouth and slipped quite neatly onto his forearm. Upon the surface of the shield was a painting of Samuligan's own face, one eye closed in a perpetual wink.

"Now you're just showing off," Deacon said, though he could not mask his tone of amazement.

Oona turned abruptly to the fireplace mantel. "All right, Deacon, please stop encouraging him before he pulls a war stallion out of his mouth next, and I am forced to battle him on horseback."

"Let's get started," said the Wizard. "Now for your first time I am going to act as an intermediary between you and the house to start your link. You will need to take my hand to do so. But once you have tapped in, you will be free to release my hand, and will remain linked until you reach the front gates."

Oona nervously placed her hand in her uncle's. The two of them stood side by side, facing Samuligan, and before she had even a moment to wonder what would happen next, she heard her uncle's voice in her head as clearly as if he had spoken directly into her ear.

"Profundus magicus!"

The surge of magic was instantaneous, as if she had been struck by lightning. And yet the experience was not a violent one. It was simply that she suddenly had access to a far greater power than she had ever experienced before. The energy and knowledge seemed endless: a vast presence, which presently belonged to her...allowing her access to an enormous library of magic in its rawest form.

She could feel the personality of it, of the house. As if

it were a person. No, not one person, but *people*. Multiple personalities ran through the magic, all of them offering up their particular strength and ability, and yet it was one magic. One source. The house. She need not have feared it, she realized now. It wanted her to use its deep powers and awaited her command. The choice was hers.

"Use only what is necessary," Uncle Alexander said from beside her and released her hand.

Oona was not sure she knew what that meant. She was still connected to the house but was unsure of what to do. Curiously, she decided to test her new powers. Pointing her wand at the cup on her uncle's desk, she uttered: *"Alum."*

She had meant only to levitate the cup, as she had done with the book at the library, but the magic that streamed from the tip of the wand caused not only the cup but everything else in the room to float off the ground, including the desk, the chair, the Wizard, and herself.

Deacon squawked in surprise as he lifted off the mantel without so much as a flutter of his wings. Only Samuligan remained rooted to the floor.

The experience took Oona so off guard that she lost focus and an instant later everything dropped back to the floor with a bang.

"Oh, dear," she said, only just managing to keep her footing. "Sorry about that, I didn't mean to..."

The Wizard braced himself against a bookshelf. "It's all right. It is vast magic you have access to, along with your own remarkable skills, not to mention that wand. That's what this is all about. Learning to control that energy. Now, try to get through that door."

Oona peered at Samuligan and for a moment she felt sorry for him. With the sheer amount of magic she had at her disposal, he did not stand a chance. The faerie grinned, as if reading her thoughts.

"Shall we dance?" he asked tauntingly.

Oona shrugged, aimed her wand and said: *"Borium."*

The spell, which was meant to shove Samuligan out of the way, only bounced off his dark suit of armor, ricocheting across the room and causing the entire fireplace to shift sideways along the wall. Deacon leapt from the mantel and fluttered to a nearby bookshelf.

"Watch where you're aiming," he said.

Oona hardly heard him. She was staring at the faerie who was wholly unaffected by the spell. At first she could not understand what went wrong. The spell had been tremendously powerful. She could still feel its after-effects.

And then it came to her, she understood. The faerie armor. She remembered how, four months ago, Red Martin had managed to get his hands on a faerie-made piece of armor: a glove that repelled all magic. And now here was Samuligan with a full suit.

How am I supposed to get past him if the magic just bounces off?

Samuligan continued to smile mockingly at her. Perhaps a spell to move him physically was the wrong kind of magic. What she needed was something to get him to step out of the way on his own.

But she knew of no such enchantment, and her frustration quickly boiled over.

"Move!" she shouted in a childish voice, and to her surprise a second spell shot from her wand. Once again the spell bounced off the armor in a jet of white light, this time colliding with the black dragon-bone desk.

The desk shuttered against the impact. It first bulged and then twisted, a roar emanating from within. Oona jumped back, startled, as the desk began to unfold. In the space of two heartbeats, the slumbering desk pulled upright, stretched out a set of bonelike wings, and raised its long neck toward the ceiling. It roared again, this time revealing its skeletal head: a dragon skull the size of a grandfather clock.

"You've awakened the dragon!" Deacon shouted, as if Oona herself had not noticed.

"I didn't mean to!" she shouted back.

"Try using *Abris neetum!*" the Wizard said quickly. "The spell that should return it to a desk."

"Ah, yes," Oona said nervously, but raising her wand, she spotted Samuligan flinch as the dragon turned in his direction.

"Or," she said, as an outrageous idea popped into her head, "I can use it."

"What?" asked both Deacon and the Wizard.

Oona had no time to explain. Taking in a huge breath to steady her nerves, she leapt onto the back of the dragon, grappled it by its spine, and pointed her wand past Samuligan.

"Through that door!" she commanded.

The dragon obeyed, sweeping Samuligan aside with one thick-boned claw and charging the door. Its skull collided with the wood, tearing the door off its hinges. Its shoulders and wings were too wide, but this did not so much as slow the beast as it tore through the wall on both sides of the doorway, leaving a gaping hole behind. Oona only just managed to cling to its clattering back, her feet pressing against the rib bones as the dragon rose to its full height within the antechamber.

"That way," Oona commanded, aiming the wand toward the front entrance. The dragon lowered its head to comply but came to a sudden halt when Samuligan vaulted through the wrecked doorway and grabbed the great beast by the tail. He jerked the tail just as the dragon tried to run, causing it to thrash violently about.

"Let go," Oona shouted at the faerie, but he seemed to be having too much fun.

Samuligan yanked hard, and the dragon swung around in an entirely new direction before slipping from his grip. It plowed forward, now heading down the side hall toward the library.

Oona screamed and ducked, just managing to avoid a

knock on the head as the beast dove down the hall, knocking pictures and candle sconces from the walls and tearing great swaths out of the enchanted carpet. It bounded down the corridor, wildly out of control, and pushed its way into the library, where they came upon a very surprised-looking Mrs. Carlyle.

The maid shrieked, diving out of the way at just the last second as the dragon crashed through the double doors into the forest of books. But suddenly, Samuligan was directly beside them. He darted in front of the beast, dropped to one knee, and raised his shield. The dragon's teeth buried themselves in the thick wood, first cracking it and then shattering it into hundreds of shards.

Springing back to his feet, Samuligan raised his gleaming sword, clearly meaning to take off the dragon's head. His eyes sparkled with a feverish intensity that Oona found both frightening and awe-inspiring. He seemed to be completely possessed by the moment, deep in his faerie nature, and Oona shuddered at the thought of an army of faeries storming through the Glass Gates with that same battle lust glinting in their enchanted eyes.

She yanked on the bones and shouted: "Back!"

The dragon reared, just avoiding the faerie's deadly blow. To her surprise, Oona found that she could control the beast by steering it with her hands. She pulled to the right and the dragon turned.

We'd better get out of the library, she thought, *before this thing starts uprooting trees and making things even more disorganized than they already are.*

She dug her heels into the rib bones, her skirt fluttering about her ankles in a jumble of petticoats, and turned the creature back toward the double doors. Once again the beast came face-to-face with Mrs. Carlyle.

The maid, who had only just regained her feet after jumping to safety, bolted so fast for the door that her shoes flew off her feet in different directions. To Oona's horror, the dragon took this as a cue to pursue.

"Oh no," she said under her breath, and then louder she shouted: "Run, Mrs. Carlyle!"

Like an overexcited dog chasing a cat through the house, the dragon plunged after the maid, Oona clinging to its back with all of her strength. The maid emerged into the central antechamber and ran toward the front door. She flung the door open so hard that it banged against the wall and bounced shut behind her. Oona could hear Mrs. Carlyle's muffled shrieks through the house's walls.

The dragon made short work of the door, crashing into it with the force of a battering ram. The door cracked down the middle, one side tearing off its hinges and flying end over end off the front porch. The beast ripped and clawed the rest of the way through the wide doorway before lunging down the front steps and into the garden. Oona could see Mrs. Carlyle running barefoot down the garden path toward the front gate in a dead panic. But out here in the open, Oona feared the dragon would easily outrun the maid.

"Stop!" she shouted, and pulled on the dragon's spine in the hopes of giving the maid more time to reach the gates.

The dragon skidded to a halt beside the rosebushes. It roared to the sky, a haunting, monstrous bellow that seemed to rattle Oona's very bones. And then Samuligan was once again in front of them, sword in hand, eyes blazing like bonfires. He placed himself between the dragon and the front gate just as Mrs. Carlyle disappeared from view.

Well, at least she's safe, Oona thought. And then she just had time to wonder *But am I?* when Samuligan brought round his sword to attack.

The dragon raised its front leg and deflected the blow, the sound like steel striking iron. It lashed out with one of its hideous claws, the black bone coming perilously close to Samuligan's unprotected face.

The faerie ducked back and then moved forward with a savage attack. Once more the dragon parried. Over and over they came at each other, their movements growing faster and faster, the sound filling the garden and Oona's skull.

She wanted it to stop. She did not want Samuligan to get hurt, and yet he would not get out of the way. *He's very good at it*, she remembered her uncle saying in regard to the faerie servant's ability to keep apprentices from the gate. It may have been more than five hundred years since his last true battle, but Samuligan did not seem to have lost his skill. She knew he would not relent and was tempted to tell the dragon to back off, when it occurred to her that dragons could do much more than run around and rampage.

"Fly!" she shouted, and aimed her wand at the beast's wings.

She had no idea if it could do so, especially considering the fact that it was a dragon made entirely of bones, with no flesh to catch the wind. But it was worth a shot. To her immense delight, the dragon responded by crouching like a giant cat and then leaping high over the faerie's head.

Her breath left her body in a cry of both fright and exhilaration as they bound into the air, the wind whipping at her hair. She clung desperately to the dragon's back, the two of them surging upward in a great curve that brought them level with the rickety tower that stuck out of the fourth floor of the house, and then took them even higher.

Oona had a moment of panic, fearful that she might fall, but just as she thought she would surely slip, the dragon banked in the opposite direction. They leveled out, giving her a breathtaking view of all of Dark Street.

It spread out before them in both directions, the glistening Glass Gates just visible some six and a half miles to the south, and the dark Iron Gates six and a half miles to the north. To the east and west, behind the line of buildings on either side of the street, there was nothing to see, just the vast expanse of nothingness known as the Drift, where Dark Street spun through the space between worlds.

Though spectacular, the view made her feel somewhat queasy, and it was not without a sense of relief that Oona pressed forward on the dragon's back and they began to descend. She considered landing outside the gates, but then remembered that the task was to reach the gates, not to get past them. She steered them to the ground, as close as possible to the gate, making sure to keep well clear of Samuligan, who remained rooted to the spot where they had left him, watching their flight.

They came down harder than she had anticipated, and this time Oona actually did lose her grip. She tumbled forward over the head of the dragon and landed in a heap of skirts on the uncut lawn. Heart in her throat, and afraid that Samuligan would beat her to it, she sprang to her feet and dashed for the gate, her hand wrapping around its cold metal frame where she sank to her knees, breath heaving in her chest.

The instant her hand touched the metal, Oona felt the magical link to the house drop away. And so, too, did the dragon, for it folded itself back into the form of the Wizard's slumbering desk.

Samuligan stuck out a long-fingered hand. "Very good, Miss Crate," he said, showing no signs of disappointment that she had beaten him.

"Yes, very good indeed," said the Wizard, who was coming down the walkway with Deacon on his shoulder. He paused beside the desk and scratched at his head. "There were, of course, less...destructive ways of achieving your task." He peered back toward the house, where the dragon's destruction could be seen quite clearly in the form of a gaping hole where the front door had once been. "But it *was* effective. And I'm sure Samuligan and Mrs. Carlyle can have things tidied up in no time."

Deacon fluttered from the Wizard's shoulder to the desk, looking at the piece of furniture wearily. He poked gingerly at the desktop with his beak before saying: "You may not *have* a maid to help clean all of this up."

"Oh," the Wizard said thoughtfully. "Good point. We do have trouble keeping good help, don't we?"

Oona threw a hand to her mouth and glanced around, as if hoping to find Mrs. Carlyle standing nearby. She peered out the gate in both directions, but the maid was nowhere to be seen.

"I hope she is all right," she said. "Probably ran home to tell Mr. Carlyle what crazy people we are. Do you think she will come back?"

She felt a twinge of sadness at the thought of Mrs. Carlyle not returning. The maid was, after all, the only female companion Oona had whom she related to.

"Oh, I'm sure she can be persuaded," the Wizard said. "Though perhaps we will set the next challenge away from the house."

Oona looked toward the ruins of the front door and laughed. "Good idea."

The Wizard peered at the massive old desk, which was slowly sinking into the lawn, and frowned. He scratched at his head as if contemplating a serious problem, and said: "Now, how do we get this monstrosity back inside?"

Chapter Five

Knots and Lies

"Never in all my life!" said Mrs. Carlyle. "I just don't know."

"But please stay, Mrs. Carlyle," Oona said. "I apologize about the dragon. It won't happen again."

They stood facing each other in the house entryway, which had been miraculously repaired by Samuligan the previous evening. The clock in the antechamber clanged, indicating that the time was nine o'clock in the morning, and Oona felt exhausted. She had slept poorly, lying awake most of the night, and when she had actually managed to fall asleep, she had dreamed of riding the wild dragon and falling from a great height.

But it had not been the flight of the dragon that had kept her up half the night. It had been the needling thought that her father's murderers were out there, back at their criminal deeds.

"Oona is quite right," the Wizard reassured Mrs. Carlyle. Only Oona, Deacon, and the Wizard greeted the maid in the entryway. Oona had requested that Samuligan remain absent for fear he would frighten Mrs. Carlyle away.

The Wizard continued: "We will have today's test in Oswald Park, miles from here, which will give you plenty of room to do your job unimpeded, Mrs. Carlyle. As you can see, Samuligan has already cleaned up our...ah...mess, so you may concentrate on your usual duties."

The maid looked skeptical. Oona had been certain that she wouldn't have shown up at all, and that she, Oona, would need to seek her out, but Mrs. Carlyle had come nevertheless, and Oona was delighted to see her dressed in her maid's uniform.

Mrs. Carlyle ran a nervous hand down the front of her apron. "And that faerie...he'll be gone with you?"

"Samuligan?" the Wizard asked. "He will be at the park as part of the battle test. You'll have the whole house to yourself."

Oona felt her stomach tighten at the thought of another test. Especially one that involved Samuligan. Not only had she dreamed half the night of falling off dragons, and the clattering sound of their moving bones, but also of the wild gleam she had seen in the faerie's eyes the day before. It had been so unnerving to witness, and Oona did not relish the idea of going toe to toe with him once again.

"Oh, and one other thing," the Wizard added. "Oona has told me of your wish to attend the Molly Morgana Moon political rally tomorrow. That will, of course, be no problem. In fact, we will all be there."

The news surprised Oona. "You are coming, Uncle? But I thought you said Molly Morgana Moon was not going to win?"

Uncle Alexander ran a wrinkled hand down his long gray beard. "That does not mean I won't show my support for what I feel is right. And who knows, I could be wrong. I have been so before and will likely be so again." He turned to the maid and cocked his head to one side, as if awaiting her decision.

"Well, all right," Mrs. Carlyle said at last, though

reluctantly. "I'll return to work...against my better judgment, mind you. Just so long as I'm not attacked again, I think we can make it work. I brought my own duster this time."

She held up her normal feather duster—one that did not giggle—and managed a faint smile. Oona smiled back, pleased to have the matter settled.

"Very good," the Wizard replied, and turned to Oona. "Three o'clock at Oswald Park then?"

Oona nodded and sighed. "I suppose I have no choice."

Her uncle crossed the antechamber toward his newly constructed study door—which Samuligan had put right the previous night—and spoke over his shoulder. "We always have a choice, Oona."

He closed the door behind him, leaving the maid, Deacon, and Oona alone in the entryway.

"He's right about that," Mrs. Carlyle said.

Oona looked at her thoughtfully. "You could have chosen not to come back."

"I might have, and don't think I didn't consider it. That dragon monstrosity nearly scared the life out of me." She sighed and looked at the feather duster. "But alas, I need the job, and I'd be hard-pressed to get paid elsewhere as much as I do here."

Oona continued to stare at her, the same thoughtful expression creasing the space between her eyes. "Would you prefer to have some other sort of job?"

Mrs. Carlyle's smile broadened. "You mean one less dangerous?" Oona's face reddened, and the maid patted her on the shoulder. "I'm just playing. I know you didn't mean to come after me with that dragon. One of the reasons I decided to come back this morning is because you're the type who learns from her mistakes, and I can trust you not to make that one twice."

Oona nodded, pleased that the maid thought so highly of her, but also embarrassed at the same time.

"I hope not," she replied.

"Let's all hope not," Deacon said. He shifted from one foot to the other on her shoulder. "Let's also hope, Miss Crate, that you learned a lesson about neglecting your research."

Oona had to will herself not to roll her eyes, because despite Deacon's insistence that they research the battle tests in order to prepare in advance, she didn't think that anything they might have found in a book would have prepared her for what had happened the previous day. And besides, she already had an idea for how she would spend her day, and it did not involve hanging out in the Pendulum House library.

She felt torn by this decision. Being prepared was something she liked to pride herself on. But with her father's killers at large—a mystery unsolved—she felt that discovering who they were and bringing them to justice must take precedence.

"Suppose I should be getting to my duties," Mrs. Carlyle said.

Oona nodded, but she could not help but satisfy her curiosity. She asked: "Would you prefer a different job?"

The maid was readjusting her white apron over her black dress. "A different line of work? Well, for a woman not born to the upper class, this is a fine enough job. Of course, women servants don't get paid as much as male servants do."

"They don't?" Oona asked, surprised. "But why?"

Mrs. Carlyle shook her head. "No reason. Just the way it is...which is why the 'way it is' needs to change. Just like we've been talking about."

Oona frowned. "Well, that needs to change right now." She spun on her heels, intent on marching straight into her uncle's study and demanding that Mrs. Carlyle be paid every cent a man would.

Mrs. Carlyle placed a hand on her shoulder. "Hold on, just now. Don't go making trouble. Your uncle pays me just fine. That's one of the reasons I returned, despite being

—

chased down the front path by some monstrous skeleton. I get paid more than most housemaids get, and likely as much as any man servant would. But elsewhere, I'm afraid the inequality is something most women have to live with."

Oona could feel herself growing angry just thinking about it. If people did the same job, she thought they should get the same pay, regardless of their gender.

Deacon twisted his head to one side—something he often did when retrieving random facts from deep within his brain. "There have been a nearly equal number of females who have held the post of Wizard as there have been males. Of course, the Magicians of Old were highly influenced by the faerie culture, where there is no clear distinction between female and male magic. In the Land of Faerie, magic is genderless."

Mrs. Carlyle shrugged. "Well, in this world, and the World of Humans beyond, things aren't so equal." She glanced at the clock. "But oh, goodness me. I need to be getting on with my work."

"Of course," Oona said as she watched the maid make her way toward the same hallway through which she had been chased the day before.

The maid hesitated at the mouth of the hallway, where several portraits still hung cockeyed against the wall. Taking in a deep breath, she straightened the frames one by one and then peered down the dim corridor, as if expecting something to jump out at her.

"I'm glad you're back," Oona said reassuringly.

"Me, too," Mrs. Carlyle said. "I think."

And with that, she disappeared down the hall.

Oona crossed her fingers superstitiously, hoping that Samuligan would not startle Mrs. Carlyle today, not even a little bit, or, despite the better pay, the maid might decide to make a permanent run for it.

The best way to make sure she was not disturbed would be to get the faerie out of the house.

"Now," Deacon said. "Shall we begin our research?"

"Indeed," Oona replied. "Samuligan?"

"You called?" The faerie stepped from behind the standing coat rack in the entryway, half startling her. Deacon cawed in surprise.

"Were you there the whole time?" Oona asked.

"I am wherever I am required," Samuligan responded in his customarily sly tone.

"Could you bring around the carriage?" Oona asked. "I should like to go downtown."

"At your service," Samuligan replied, and with a deep bow headed out the front door.

"But I thought we were doing research," Deacon squawked.

"We are, Deacon," Oona said. "We are going to find out who the Rose Thieves are. We're going to find out who killed my father."

Pedestrians moved about the sidewalk and carriages clattered down the street. On this bright and clear day, the pointy-hat-shaped library cast a shadow across the street to where Oona stood in front of the Dark Street Theater.

Arms folded, she stood beside the ironwork joke-telling clock, upon which a flyer had been posted announcing Molly Morgana Moon's Thursday political rally at Oswald Park. Oona hardly noticed it. She was too busy staring at the museum steps, attempting to imagine how the thieves snuck up on the night watchman.

A mechanical voice sounded from within the clock: "Why did the wild pig cross the road?"

"I don't know," sounded a second, equally mechanical voice. "Why *did* the wild pig cross the road?"

The first voice replied: "He wanted to get away from

his friends...they were all *boars!*"

"Terrible," Deacon said. *"Bore* and *boar* aren't even spelled the same."

"That's the point, Deacon," Oona said absently. "That's what makes it amusing."

"If you say so," Deacon said.

But Oona was hardly paying attention to their conversation, let alone the clock and its ridiculous sense of humor. Her attention was fixed upon the museum door. She remembered what she had overheard the night watchman telling Inspector White, about the woman running up the steps. Clearly, the woman had been a diversion meant to distract the guard, giving the male thief time to sneak up behind and knock the watchman on the head. At night the building was not well lit. The man could easily have been lying in wait close by.

"The thieves likely knew that the guard took his snack break at the same time every night," Oona said. "They were waiting for him. It was well planned."

"Indeed," Deacon said, "which is precisely what you need for this afternoon's battle test. A plan."

"Oh, I think she handled herself quite all right without preparation," Samuligan said from atop the nearby carriage. He wiggled his fingers in display of the red line that ran across the back of his hand in a great slash. "I have the scar to prove it."

"See, Deacon," Oona said. "Samuligan thinks I did well."

"Of course he's saying that," Deacon chided. "He doesn't want you to be prepared for your next challenge. He's your opponent."

Oona raised an eyebrow. "Is that true, Samuligan? Will I be facing you once again today, or will it be something different?"

The faerie pulled his cowboy hat down over his eyes and shrugged.

"You see," Deacon said. "He's no help. We should be back in the Pendulum House library, researching."

Oona knew he was right. Yesterday's test had turned out to be far more demanding than she had expected, and yet her instincts were telling her that the more important thing to do was to find those responsible for taking her father away—taking his life—and to make sure they paid for it. She did not, however, want to say so out loud, as she was sure that Deacon would not understand.

She was convinced that, unless someone had experienced it for themselves, it was impossible truly to understand what it was like to know that your father—the man who was supposed to care for you and keep you safe—had been murdered, and that his killers where still out there. It was impossible to know the emptiness that came with never again feeling your hero's arms wrap around you, or kiss you good night, not to mention the frustration of knowing that the police department was too incompetent to capture the culprits.

She was happy to change the topic. "Look, Deacon, it's Mr. Bop."

"So it is," he replied rather dryly, as if detecting the purpose of her dramatic shift of subject.

An enormous man was exiting the building next door to the museum. He made his way across the street in Oona's direction. The closer he came, the easier it was to see the mask of squiggly tattoos that inked every surface of his broad face—a clear reminder that Mr. Bop was a prominent member of the Magicians Legal Alliance. A top hat rested precariously atop his bald head, and for such a giant of a man Mr. Bop moved quite gracefully.

He hopped up onto the curb, which Oona felt tremble slightly beneath her feet, and tipped his hat.

"Hello, Miss Crate," he said amiably.

A thought occurred to Oona. "Mr. Bop, might I have a word?"

66

He came to a halt and whirled round on one heel like a great big globe that someone had given a spin.

"We can have more than one, if you like," he said. His genuine smile reached nearly to his bushy side-whiskers, and Oona detected that he smelled faintly of cupcakes. "Such marvelous questions you always ask, Miss Crate. Tell me, have you reconsidered joining the society?"

The question vexed Oona at first, and it took her a moment to remember that, some months ago, Mr. Bob had revealed that he belonged to the highly mysterious—and ridiculously irrational—Tick-Tock Society...an organization so secretive that even its own members did not know who each other were.

"To tell the truth, I haven't given it much thought," Oona said, not wanting to put him off.

But Mr. Bop seemed to be a hard man to put off. He continued to smile broadly, his jowls jiggling beneath multiple chins. "Quite all right. Just thought I'd ask. Let's just forget I mentioned it, shall we? How may I be of assistance?"

Oona gestured across the street, toward the building from which Mr. Bop had exited. "You live there, don't you, Mr. Bop? Next door to the museum and above Madame Iree's Boutique?"

She knew that he did, having established this fact on a previous case.

"I do," he replied. "And if you are wondering about the break-in that happened last night, you should know that after the incident with the witches breaking a hole through the wall of the dress shop into the museum, the curator had large sheets of metal installed along the museum walls, all around, to prevent such an event occurring again."

Oona nodded. The museum renovations had been highly publicized to prevent anyone else from attempting a similar crime. This time there was no question how the culprits had entered the museum—they had knocked out the night watchman and entered and exited through the front door. But that didn't mean they had done so unobserved.

Oona stepped away from the iron clock. "Do you remember seeing or hearing anything strange happen around nine o'clock Monday night? Through the window of your apartment perhaps?"

Mr. Bop's smile shrank, and his tattooed eyebrows drew closer together, as if he were remembering something quite unpleasant.

"You did, didn't you?" Oona asked excitedly.

But Mr. Bop shook his head. "Oh no. Sorry, but I wasn't even home at nine o'clock on Monday night. I was at my competitive cooking class, like I am every Monday and Wednesday night."

"Competitive cooking class?" Deacon asked. "What on earth is that?"

Mr. Bop's smile disappeared all together. "It is a highly competitive class where students learn the art of cooking from the world-renowned culinary genius Chef Raymond Rude."

Oona was perplexed. "Don't you like the class?"

Mr. Bop's eyes went wide at the suggestion. "My dear, it is my favorite part of the week! It's just that, after each class our plate is judged by a panel of food experts, who taste all of the dishes and declare a winner. And on Monday night I created perhaps the most delicious chicken fricassée ever served on Dark Street. And that is not just my opinion. Even Chef Rude said it was brilliant, and he never says anything like that. Believe me, he's not just called Chef *Rude* because that is his last name."

Oona shook her head, confused. "Well, I don't know what chicken fricassée tastes like, but it sounds like you should be proud of yourself."

"But that's just the thing," Mr. Bop explained. "It doesn't matter what I think. It's what the *critics* think that matters, and all of the food judges agreed that the chicken was perfectly cooked...all except one. Miss Mary Shusher said it was too dry. Mary Shusher is always quite hard to please, everyone knows that...but dry? My chicken? Never. So I told her exactly what I thought, and...and unfortunately, arguing with the judges is not allowed, and I was disqualified. The winning dish went to Miss Isadora Iree instead."

Oona's eyebrows shot up at the mention of Adler's sister. It was hard to imagine the pampered, arrogant Isadora Iree in a cooking class.

Remembering her own experience with Mary Shusher, Oona felt the need to console Mr. Bop. "You know, my uncle Alexander, who is quite wise, says it's more important that *you* love what you do than that other people—" But Oona abruptly stopped. A realization occurred to her. "Did you say that Mary Shusher was at your cooking class on Monday night? Are you sure?"

Mr. Bop nodded, his jowls jiggling vigorously. "Of course I'm sure. I kept thinking about it all day yesterday."

Oona turned to Deacon. "And yet when I spoke with her yesterday, Mary said that she was at home at nine o'clock with her grandmother."

Deacon took in a sharp breath. "By Oswald, you're right!"

Oona peered up at the hat-shaped library across the street. "She lied."

"But why?" Deacon asked. "If she had a legitimate alibi for the time of the crime, why would she try to hide it?"

Oona began to stride diagonally across the street in the direction of the museum. "Let's find out, shall we?"

"It was nice talking to you, Miss Crate," Mr. Bop called after her. "Thanks for trying to cheer me up."

Oona darted quickly between two moving carriages— causing one of the horses to whinny and a driver to shout something indiscernible at her—before reaching the other side of the street.

"Well, that was rather rude," Deacon chastised from her shoulder.

"What?" Oona asked, and glanced vaguely back toward the street. "Yes, who was that who shouted at me?"

"I was referring to *you*," Deacon said. "You didn't even say good-bye to Mr. Bop."

"Oh," Oona said, and stopped on the third museum step. She turned and raised a hand, meaning at least to give Mr. Bop a wave, but he was already heading back up the street. "Well, I'll apologize next time I see him."

She stared for a moment at the theater across the street. An idea came to her, and she felt a surge of excitement. Why she hadn't thought of it the day before, she did not know. She thrust a finger in the air and resumed her stride up the stone steps. "Come along, Deacon. Let's see what excuse Mary Shusher has for her lie."

"Mary's not in today," Adler said. "She's got the day off."

He leaned on the reference desk, his threadbare top hat cockeyed on his head, frayed bits of cloth dangling from the brim. Oona had yet to see him without it.

"I see," Oona said, and then in her best library whisper told Adler what she had learned from Mr. Bop.

"So Mary lied," Adler said quietly. "I wonder why."

Oona leaned over the counter. "I don't know. But Mr. Bop said that his competitive cooking class takes place every Monday and Wednesday."

Adler looked thoughtful as he bent forward, their faces now quite close. Oona's pulse quickened.

"You know, my sister's in that class," he said. "All the girls at the Academy of Fine Young Ladies are supposed to engage in extracurricular activities. Most of 'em go for dancing lessons, or piano, but Isadora liked the idea of competitive cooking. I don't think it was so much the cooking part but the competitive bit that attracted her."

Oona rolled her eyes. She knew from personal experience just how competitive Isadora Iree could be. The girl had tried to cheat her way to victory in the Magician's Tower Contest and had still been quite a poor loser when Oona had come out victorious.

Oona leaned in even closer, batting her eyes. "Well, Mr. Bop gave the impression that Mary is a regular judge. I was just thinking, if you know where the cooking class is, we could show up there tonight and...question Mary Shusher...together."

The two of them stared at each other for a long moment, and Deacon jumped uncomfortably from Oona's shoulder onto the countertop.

Adler glanced at the raven, blinking like a boy coming out of a daze. Finally, he said: "Sorry, I can't."

Oona pulled away from the counter, wondering if it had been too bold to ask him to go somewhere so late at night.

Adler cleared his throat. "It's just that I have that really big test tomorrow at the alliance—the one I told you about—and I really need to study tonight so I can pass."

"Ah, yes," Oona said awkwardly.

"Which is precisely what Miss Crate should be doing right now," Deacon said. "Studying."

Oona felt a knot twist in her stomach. She knew Deacon was right.

"I do still plan on attending the rally tomorrow," Adler said.

"Yes, of course," Oona said.

"Anyway," Adler said, "the class takes place at the Culinary Institute on the Lower North End."

Oona nodded. "I'm sure Samuligan will be able to find it." Again that uncomfortable silence. And then Oona remembered the brainstorm she'd had on the museum steps while looking at the theater across the street.

"Can you show me your books on theater craft?"

"Theater craft?" Adler said. "Sure. Why the sudden interest in thea—" he paused, his eyes going wide. "Of course! There's bound to be descriptions of knots in books on theater. They've got all kinds of ropes and pulleys they use backstage. You think maybe the Rose Thieves worked in the theater, and that's where they learned to tie that fancy knot?"

"It's worth a shot," Oona said.

They hurried to the third-floor balcony, where they found a vast selection of books on theater. Oona couldn't help but feel daunted by the sheer volume of books written on the subject, but Adler quickly explained that the majority of the books were plays to be performed, and books on the art of directing and acting. What they were looking for were books on the actual backstage craftwork and the construction of stage sets. It turned out there was a specific section for this, and Oona's appreciation for the organization of the public library grew immensely.

"Here," he said, pulling several books from the shelves and handing them to Oona. He pulled another pile and tucked them under his arm. "And these as well."

Oona knelt down to open one of the books, but Adler had a different idea.

"Come on," he said. "There's better light back downstairs."

"Oh, all right," Oona said, wondering if Adler was just making an excuse to be somewhere less private.

Back at the reference area, they laid the books out on a table and began their search. Oona found no reference to knots at all in the first book she looked at, *Theater Dreams: Bringing Imagination to Life*, by Horton Hob, and was hoping to have better luck with *The Stages of Life: Understanding the Craft of Theatrical Space*, by Gordon Glibbit Jr., when the door behind the reference counter opened and Mrs. Shusher the librarian stepped out of her office and approached the reference counter.

Oona noted how the librarian was dressed in the same black lab coat she had been wearing the day before. Mrs. Shusher glanced toward the large clock on the wall. Adler jumped to his feet, as if to hurry back to his book sorting, but he stopped when a tall, thin man entered the library through the main doors and proceeded directly to the reference counter.

"That's Mr. Shusher," Adler whispered. "Mrs. Shusher's husband."

"Mary's father," Oona said.

Adler nodded. "I've only seen him once before, when he came in about a week ago. Not a very nice man, if you ask me. Told me who he was and that he wanted to see his wife right away. I put out my hand and introduced myself, and he looked at me as if I had just spit on his shoe. Oh aye, and so he just walks around the counter and calls through the door: 'Mrs. Shusher, it's me, Mr. Shusher.' And she yells back: 'Come in, Mr. Shusher!' And he goes in, leaving me with my hand sticking out like a dolt."

Oona watched Mr. Shusher approach the counter. Though smartly dressed in a crisp suit and an expensive bowler hat, his cleanly shaved face gave the appearance of being worn. Crow's-feet lined the corners of his eyes, and his mouth was turned down at the ends. He seemed the type of person whose face had settled into a permanent frown, and Oona could see why Adler was reluctant to approach the counter.

"Hello, Mr. Shusher," the librarian said in a hushed voice.

"Mrs. Shusher," the man replied, removing his hat and holding it in his hands.

"Is everything settled?" she asked.

"Oh yes. Took care of it this morning after you left."

"Hidden?"

Mr. Shusher spun his hat on his finger. "Where no one would ever think to look."

"Perfect. Now I—" She stopped speaking and turned her head to look at Oona and Adler, both of whom were staring back at her.

Oona quickly looked down at the book in front of her.

"Mr. Iree," Mrs. Shusher said, her voice somehow soft and authoritative at the same time. She gestured to the books on the cart. "Are these all organized?"

Adler took in an audible gulp. "I...ah...Miss Crate here needed help finding some books."

Oona looked up. Both Mr. and Mrs. Shusher were looking at her.

Mrs. Shusher placed her hand on the sorting cart. "It seems she has found the books, Mr. Iree, so now you may return to your duties."

"Yes, of course," Adler replied, and made his way back to the cart.

Mrs. Shusher turned back to her husband. "Would you like to stay for lunch, Mr. Shusher?"

He shook his head. "No time, Mrs. Shusher. I'll see you at home."

He turned to go.

Mrs. Shusher said: "Don't forget about the meeting tonight."

"Wouldn't dream of it," he said, and then disappeared through the library doors.

Mrs. Shusher closed her office door behind her.

Oona approached the counter and whispered: "Don't you think it's kind of strange that they call each other Mr. and Mrs. Shusher, even though they are married?"

Adler shrugged. "People are different."

"That is true," Oona said, "but what intrigues me even more is what they were hiding."

Adler cast a look over his shoulder toward the hidden door. "I don't know, but they sure clammed up when they realized we were listening."

Oona nodded. She couldn't help but imagine Mr. Shusher removing a red ruby from his pocket and burying it in a hole somewhere, or perhaps slipping it into a vase.

"Of course, they could have been talking about anything," Adler whispered.

"True. But what could they be—" Oona stopped speaking as a thought came to her, a memory from the previous day.

"Shush, he'll hear you," she said.

"Who'll hear me?" Adler asked.

Oona shook her head. "No. Those are the words the night watchman heard the female thief say to the male thief. The guard heard her say: 'Shush, he'll hear you."

"Oh, I see," Adler said, looking confused.

Oona could feel her arms begin to tingle with the excitement of discovering a clue. "What if the night watchman misheard the thief? What if the male thief actually said: '*Mrs. Shusher*, he'll hear you'?"

Adler's eyes went wide. "There's something."

Oona was nodding. "Yes, but we need proof."

"Maybe you'll find something about the Rose Knot in those theater books, and you can use it to tie the Shushers to the crime...no pun intended."

Deacon laughed from Oona's shoulder. "Very good, Mr. Iree. *Tie* them to the crime."

But Oona did not smile. She wasn't so sure that looking through the books was the best course of action. She was more inclined to follow Mr. Shusher and see if he might lead her to this elusive hiding place, but now it was too late. He was already gone, and it would be difficult to find him on the busy street.

And then, of course, there was the matter of why Mary Shusher had lied about her whereabouts on the night of the theft.

Perhaps they are all in on it together, she thought.

—

It occurred to her that these people just might be the very criminals who had murdered her father, and a cold sensation washed over her. She blinked several times, trying to clear her head. "Well, we are here. Let's finish going through those books."

"I'll have to leave that to you, Miss Crate," Adler said, and cocked a thumb over his shoulder toward the librarian's door.

The fact that he had used her last name did not escape her. She sighed. "Then I guess it's up to you and me, Deacon. Let's find that knot."

Chapter Six

The Second Test

Not a single reference to the notorious Rose Knot was to be found in the books on theater craft, and by the time they had searched through all of them, it was nearly three o'clock.

"We'll be late," Deacon said.

The two of them made a dash for it, descending both the library and museum steps two at a time. Samuligan waited dutifully for her atop the carriage to take them to the park. Ten minutes and one wild carriage ride later, Oona stepped to the curb at the park entrance.

Dressed in his long purple robes, Uncle Alexander was waiting for them beside the open gate. He nodded pleasantly to the people passing by, all of whom seemed quite interested to see the Wizard out and about. Oona considered him for a moment, this man whom had become like a father to her. Her guardian and teacher.

There was a slight sadness about his eyes that only the most astute observer might notice. Oona had seen that sadness in the reflection of her own face not too long ago, and yet the look had been a part of her uncle for as long as she had known him. Since even before the family deaths that had so affected them both. She wondered briefly where it came from.

Her uncle had been a single man for his entire life, she knew. Married to his work. She wondered if he had ever been in love. It was a question she had never thought to ask.

"Hello, Uncle," Oona said.

"Ah, there you are," he said. "Come along. We're off to the pond."

"Isn't Samuligan coming?" Oona asked, and she cast a look over her shoulder toward the driver's seat of the carriage. But Samuligan was nowhere to be found.

"He'll be along," the Wizard said unconcernedly.

Oona, however, was quite concerned, and she glanced warily around as they made their way toward the large sailing pond. She couldn't help but wonder where the faerie servant might be lurking, and what mischief he had up his enchanted sleeve.

The Magician's Tower was long gone, having been torn down after the contest, and the center of the park was once again nothing but a wide-open field of grass—a place where there had once been a tree. The tree had, of course, been *the* tree, an enormous fig that had fallen over three years ago in a fiery burst, crushing the life from Oona's mother and sister as they sat beneath its shade and watched Oona perform her magic. The thought of performing magic here once again was daunting, and the fear of causing another catastrophe danced in and out of her mind like a mischievous sprite.

She shoved the thought aside, choosing instead to remind herself that another incident had happened here not so long ago...a certain kiss. The thought emboldened her.

"Have you ever been in love, Uncle?" she asked quite daringly.

The Wizard came to an abrupt halt, blinking several times as if the question had confused him.

He turned to her, a quizzical look on his face. "Why do

you ask?"

Her face reddened, and she could only shrug. She certainly did not wish to disclose her feelings about Adler Iree. Not yet.

The Wizard peered at her for what seemed like a long moment...though in truth he seemed to be looking *through* her more than *at* her. Lost in memory.

"I have known love," he said at last. "I experience it every day...though I suspect you mean, have I ever been *in* love with someone else. To that, I will simply say yes, but now is not the time to discuss old sweethearts. Come along."

He once again took up his decisive stride, and Oona hurried to keep up, her mind racing with curiosity over whom the Wizard's sweetheart might have been, and what had happened to her.

Not far from the spot where the tower had stood, Oona could see preparations being made for Molly Morgana Moon's campaign rally. A stage had been erected, and a sign exclaiming MOLLY MORGANA MOON FOR STREET COUNCIL hung between two trees.

Oona peered hard at the sign, thinking that it would be just like Samuligan to hide up there, forming himself into one of the letters on the sign or some such strangeness. But if he was there, she could not make him out, and they reached the edge of the pond without incident. Deacon's head turned this way and that, as if he, too, were concerned about Samuligan's whereabouts.

"We begin today's test where we left off yesterday," her uncle explained. "I will once again help you access the powers of Pendulum House, and this time you will use the magic to defend this."

He pulled from his pocket a shiny metal ball.

"This," he continued, "represents the World of Man." Oona gave him a discerning look, and he held up his other hand as if surrendering. "All right, the World of *Humans*. Whichever you prefer. Anyway, when I say the word,

79

Samuligan will have precisely three tries to get past you and get this."

The Wizard placed the fist-sized metal ball on the ground where the grass met the edge of the water.

Oona looked eagerly around, expecting Samuligan to step from behind a nearby tree, but still, the faerie was nowhere to be seen.

She peered down at the ball, and a thought occurred to her. "How am I to connect with Pendulum House when we are miles away?"

Uncle Alexander raised an eyebrow at Deacon.

Deacon shifted uneasily on Oona's shoulder. "I assure you, sir, I did teach her about such things."

Oona started in surprise. "You did? Well, it must have been a long time ago, because I have no recollection of it."

"It was one year ago, to be precise," Deacon said knowingly. "But at the time, you had very little interest in magic, and were planning on giving it up completely."

Oona's gaze shifted briefly toward the center of the park, and she felt a tightening in her stomach.

"Nevertheless," her uncle said, and spread his hands wide. "The Wizard may access the house's magic wherever he or she goes, so long as it is done on Dark Street. Now, take this in your wand hand." He once again handed her Oswald's wand.

Oona felt nervous about having the wand out in the open. It was a very powerful magical object that Red Martin himself had tried to take from her.

Seeming to sense her unease, the Wizard said: "Don't worry. While you are linked to the house, no one besides an extremely powerful magician or faerie would have a chance of taking it away...and Red Martin, as you know, is no magician."

"But Samuligan is a powerful faerie," Oona said.

Her uncle smiled. "And he may very well try to take it away from you. With him, you never know. Now take my hand with your free hand, and I will once again help you link with the house. Do you remember the incantation?"

Oona nodded, giving Deacon a sideways glance. "That, I do remember." She took in a breath, and uttered: "*Profundus magicus!*"

The sensation of connecting to an immense magical force was instant. And so was Samuligan's attack.

He shot up out of the pond, his long black cloak and cowboy hat scattering water in every direction. Covered in moss and slime, Samuligan darted toward the pond's edge, where the metal ball lay vulnerable and defenseless.

The World of Humans! Oona thought. *He's going to get it before I've even started.*

But in that same instant, something else occurred inside of her. Not a thought...at least not her own. It was the power of the house pouring into her, and she suddenly understood that she did not need to think of something to do, because the house was going to think of something for her.

She raised the wand as Samuligan came splashing to the edge of the pond, his long faerie fingers groping for the metal sphere. She acted on instinct—or on the *house's* instinct—it was terribly confusing to try to differentiate between the two.

She turned the wand upward toward her shoulder so that its tip touched Deacon's chest. He cawed in surprise as Oona shouted: *"Ani voxsis!"*

With a harrowing cry, Deacon launched from her shoulder like a bullet, claws engaged. He latched onto Samuligan's wrist and hurtled upward.

Oona flicked her wand and Deacon soared toward the sky, Samuligan dangling beneath him. They flew high into the air and hovered just above the tops of the trees, and it occurred to Oona that the magic was imbuing Deacon with supernatural powers. No normal raven could possibly lift a six-and-a-half-foot-tall faerie from the ground, and as she watched Samuligan struggle to free himself from the raven's iron grip, she noticed an aura of light surrounding Deacon. The light radiated from his wings in shimmering rays of yellow against the purple-blue sky.

She raised the wand above her head, whirling it in a circle, and Deacon followed the looping pattern, gaining speed. Tracers of light jetted out behind him like ribbons. Samuligan's boots flew off in different directions, yet his cowboy hat remained remarkably secure upon is head.

At last Oona gave her wand a second flick and shouted: *"Fanissium!"*

Deacon's shimmery glow vanished, and his claws disengaged from the faerie's wrist. Samuligan went flying. He tumbled through the air before landing quite nimbly in the topmost branches of a nearby tree. His eyes twinkled, his toothy grin as wide as the moon as he looked down at her and held up one finger.

"One try down," the Wizard said, sounding quite pleased. "Very good, Oona. That was quick thinking, to enchant Deacon."

Deacon settled himself on a low branch and ruffled his feathers. "You might have asked first!"

Oona shook her head. "Sorry, Deacon, but there was no time. And besides, I can't say for sure that it was me who thought of it."

The Wizard's bushy eyebrows rose slightly, and Oona thought she detected a smile. "Yes, sometimes the house can act of its own accord, doing what it believes best. It brings up the question of who is the master, the magic or the magician. But that is a philosophical debate for another time. Samuligan still has two more tries to get past you. Remember, the World of Man is relying on you."

"The World of *Humans*," Oona said.

She glanced back toward the top of the tree to where Samuligan had landed catlike upon the upper-most branches. He was nowhere to be seen.

"That scoundrel," Oona said. "Where has he gotten to?"

All seemed silent. Across the pond, she could make out what appeared to be several couples lounging on picnic blankets and staring in her direction. They had no doubt noticed the incident with Samuligan and were keen to see what was going to happen next. So was Oona. She tensed, casting anxious looks in every direction.

And then she heard it, a woman speaking very loudly. At first Oona could not make out what the voice was saying, but it was definitely getting louder, getting closer.

Oona whirled around and peered down the paved pedestrian path that led from the front gate to the pond. Coming down the path was a woman in a long white dress riding a bicycle. The feather in her hat wafted wildly in the breeze, and as she approached, Oona realized that the woman was riding quite fast.

As if responding to Oona's thought, the woman cried: "Too fast! We are going much too fast!"

Oona's face pinched in confusion. What did the woman mean by *we*?

And then the bicycle turned slightly, and Oona understood perfectly what the woman had meant. It was not a one-seater but a two-seater bicycle. The only reason Oona had not been able to tell earlier was because the bike was coming straight at her, and the rider on the rear seat was hunched over behind the woman and pedaling like a madman.

Except that's no man, Oona thought. *It's a faerie.*

And she understood all too quickly what Samuligan was up to. Knowing that Oona would be reluctant to perform a powerful spell for fear of hitting an innocent pedestrian, he was using the woman as a kind of shield.

———

"When I said we could share the bike," the woman called back to Samuligan in a high-pitched, panicky voice, "I thought you meant for a leisurely ride! Now please slow down, sir, or we'll end up in the pond!"

But Samuligan did not slow down. If anything, his long faerie legs began pumping harder, and Oona had a suspicion that ending up in the pond, right next to the metal ball, was precisely what he had in mind, regardless of sending the frightened woman and the bike into the muddy waters.

"Oh, dear, this can't be good," Oona heard her uncle say beside her. He raised his wand, clearly meaning to stop Samuligan from going too far, but Oona put up her hand.

"No, Uncle, I have this," she said, and aimed her wand at the bike tires. She waited.

"Now would be a good time," her uncle advised her, and she could hear the tension in his voice.

"Wait," Oona said. She continued to track the wheels with the tip of her wand, turning as the bicycle approached.

"Oh, dear, we're going to crash!" the woman cried.

The front tire came up even with the water and Oona caught a glimpse of Samuligan's grin from beneath his hat.

"Alabarium!" she called.

It was not a spell that she had ever used before. Indeed, like the spell she had used on Deacon, she had not even known that it existed. It was the knowledge and power of Pendulum House that provided her with just the right spell for the occasion, and Oona had to admit, it was quite brilliant.

Light sprayed from the tip of her wand and struck the tire, which morphed instantly into a curved hull. The entire bicycle transformed as it hit the water, changing from metal frame to wooden boat in the blink of an eye. A sail popped up between Samuligan and the woman in white, and before Samuligan could make a leap for the metal ball, Oona raised her wand and called: *"Wind!"*

The sail immediately filled with a burst of air so strong that the ship shot across the surface of the pond like a sled on ice. The observing couples across the water were suddenly scrambling to get out of the way as the boat slid out of the water and came to a stop on top of one of the picnic blankets.

Oona could hear the woman in white shout several rather rude names at Samuligan as he climbed leisurely out of the boat. The man whose blanket the boat was presently resting on seemed to have something to say about the matter as well, but Samuligan ignored them all, and instead turned to face Oona from across the water, holding up two fingers.

"That's two down," the Wizard said, clearly relieved.

Oona exhaled, realizing that she had been holding her breath for quite some time.

"One to go," she said.

This time, she told herself, *I won't take my eyes off him.*

But when something shiny moved at her feet, Oona couldn't help herself. The metal ball all at once rose to shoulder height, hovering briefly, tauntingly before her. She grabbed at it with her hand, but the instant she did so the ball shot across the pond toward Samuligan's outstretched hand.

Her reaction came quick as lightning. Wand raised, she called: *"Hovarium!"*

A streak of purple light shot from the end of the wand, striking the ball as it raced through the air. The metal sphere stopped just out of Samuligan's reach and then slowly reversed its direction, returning to Oona.

"Morium!" Samuligan cried in a low, guttural voice. The ball stopped and then once again moved toward the faerie's coaxing arms. His hands moved in a "come here" gesture, as if assuring the ball that he was its master.

With her own spell still connected to the sphere, she could sense the might of the faerie's magic, and she had a feeling that he wasn't even giving it his all. He was playing with her. But according to her intuition, she and Pendulum

---

85

House had far more magic as well.

"*Morium,*" she called, increasing her own spell's power just as Samuligan had done, and the ball once more began to return to her.

"*Morium!*" Samuligan cried again, and the ball switched directions.

"*Morium,*" she called back.

And so it became a tug-of-war, with the ball being pulled first one direction, and then another, each time the opposing forces increasing until Oona's mind began to feel like soup. Her arm began to ache, her grip on the wand increasing, and it soon felt as if she were slipping away, the magic taking her over completely.

The enchantment intensified to a fevered pitch, charging the air above the water, where thin bolts of white and purple lightning arced off the ball, striking the surface of the pond. A smell of sulfur infused the air, hitting Oona's nose on an electrically charged breeze, and still she held on, determined to save the World of Humans from the diabolical faerie.

That's when she saw Samuligan waver on the far side of the water. He staggered forward and dropped to one knee. Oona took in a sharp breath and immediately released her spell, alarmed that she might have injured the faerie.

The ball simply hovered over the center of the pond.

"Samuligan, are you all right?" Oona shouted.

Samuligan glanced up from his kneeling position...and grinned. Oona groaned at her own stupidity as the faerie snapped his fingers and the ball shot like a bullet toward his open hand.

He wasn't hurt, she realized. *He was just pretending because he knew I would be concerned for him.*

It was a clever and dirty trick, and a clever trick demanded an even cleverer bit of retribution.

Again, it was as if she didn't need to think about what to do. The magic guided her—the house's seemingly infinite wisdom—and with a motion much like the flicking of a whip, Oona shot her mind out the tip of the wand and sent it into the ball.

"Akvis!"

Suddenly, she *was* the ball. Her body may have been standing on the far side of the pond, but presently she was flying through the air toward Samuligan's outstretched hand. It was the most extraordinary and bizarre magic she had ever experienced. For one panicky moment she had a fear that she might not be able to get back...that she would be stuck inside of this metal ball forever, but the thought passed as quickly as it had come. There was no time to do anything but think: *Up!*

And up she went, heading straight for the sky and beyond. She had a feeling that if she did not change directions she would eventually strike the moon.

To me, she thought, which was a strange thought to have because presently she *was* the ball. What was even stranger was that she heard her own voice shout "To me!" from below, and had she still been connected to her body, she might have shaken her head at the confusion it caused.

Regardless, she began to plummet in the direction of her body's outspread hand. As she fell, another voice seemed to fill her up.

"Come to me," it said in a lulling, sly tone. Oona knew that voice. It was Samuligan once more trying to regain control of the ball, but now that she had planted her mind inside the sphere, Samuligan did not have a chance of controlling it. She was in control, and she would decide the fate of the world.

And then it was over. The ball slapped into Oona's palm, and her mind returned to her body. She staggered, disoriented, swinging her hands out at her sides for balance. Lucky for her, a set of strong hands caught her before she fell.

Looking around, she discovered that it was Samuligan

who had prevented her fall. How he had gotten from the far side of the pond to right behind her so quickly she did not know, but she was glad he was there. He helped her back to her feet and then held up three fingers.

"And that makes three," the Wizard said, sounding quite pleased.

"Three indeed," Samuligan said, raising his eyebrows so that they disappeared beneath the brim of his hat. "You know, I do believe you are the first apprentice to best me at all three attempts in nearly three hundred years."

Oona blinked several times, still trying to reorient herself with her body. She glanced down at the metal ball in her hand. "You mean that other apprentices have failed some of the tests?"

The Wizard placed a hand on her shoulder. "Of course. If you had researched the tests in the Pendulum House library, you might have known that most of the apprentices have failed many of the tests. When I was an apprentice, I believe Samuligan got the ball from me on his second try...and he wasn't even using a pedestrian as a human shield."

The Wizard eyed the faerie disapprovingly, and Samuligan gave a little bow.

"Now get back over here, you hooligan!" they all heard a far-off voice call. They turned to discover the woman in white standing in the boat across the pond, red in the face, one hand on her hip. She pointed in Samuligan's direction. "Get over here and turn this boat back into a bicycle!"

Even Oona found the woman to be somewhat of a comical sight. Remembering that it was she, Oona, and not Samuligan who had transfigured the bicycle, she met the faerie's gaze, and the tension from the battle suddenly melted away. He placed a hand on her shoulder, and the two of them burst out laughing.

"It's no laughing matter!" the woman called indignantly from across the water. "This bike is a rental, and

I'd very much like to get my deposit back!"

Chapter Seven

The Perfect Bite

"You are still planning on visiting the Culinary Institute?" Deacon asked. He stood upon Oona's dressing table, where scattered papers lay messily across the wood surface.

Oona had just finished changing into her evening attire, a green dress trimmed with white lace. She fastened the front buttons and looked herself over in the mirror.

"I think maybe I should have chosen the black dress. I would be less conspicuous in black, and I wish to observe, not *be* observed."

"Then your answer is *yes*, I take it?" Deacon asked.

Oona gave him a measured look. "Of course I'm planning on going to the cooking class, Deacon. How else am I to find out why Mary Shusher lied about her whereabouts on the night of the theft?"

"You could ask her tomorrow at the library," Deacon reasoned.

Oona grabbed a pair of black gloves from off her bed and turned toward the door. "I want to surprise her, catch her in the very place that she did not want us to know about."

Deacon flew to her shoulder. "How do you know she

did not want you to know about it?"

Oona started down the hallway, slipping her fingers into the gloves. "Mary Shusher intentionally told us that she was home with her grandmother when she was actually at the cooking school. There has got to be a reason why she lied."

"Either way, she has an alibi for the night of the theft of the Faerie Carbuncle," Deacon pointed out, as the two of them descended the curving staircase to the first floor.

The smell of wood and dust infused the air, yet there was another smell as well...a subtler smell that Oona had failed to notice before. It was the permeating smell of magic. Ever since she had linked with the house the day before, she had become aware of the ever-present smell. Indeed, she had never even known that magic had a smell, but now that she did smell it, she realized that it had always been there, filling up the rooms and the hallways with its hidden sent.

She glanced at the clock on the wall. It was eight thirty. The cooking class started at nine.

"Samuligan?" she called.

"Yes?" he replied.

Oona peered around the antechamber but did not see him. Something above her moved, and she looked up, startled.

"Samuligan, what on earth are you doing up there?" she asked.

Samuligan, who was presently hanging upside down from the chandelier, looked surprised, as if he'd had no idea of his whereabouts until she pointed it out. But Oona had lived with the faerie servant too long to be fooled. He knew exactly where he was and what he was doing.

"Anyway," Oona said, attempting to ignore the faerie's high jinks, "I need you to bring around the carriage."

"Ah, but I have already brought it around, Miss Crate," Samuligan said. "It sits at the curb even now, waiting to take us to the Culinary Institute."

He somersaulted through the air, landing catlike upon

the floor, and then bounded forward to open the door. Oona followed. As she climbed into the carriage, she turned to Deacon, who had perched himself upon the opposite seat. "What was it you were asking, Deacon?"

Overhead, they could hear Samuligan slap at the reins. The carriage turned north in the direction of the Iron Gates.

Deacon steadied himself against the motion of the carriage before answering. "I was saying that no matter how you look at it, Mary Shusher could not be the thief because she already has an alibi."

"Then why did she lie?" Oona asked.

"I don't know," Deacon said. "But I'm beginning to think that you are simply trying to get back at her for criticizing your abilities yesterday."

Oona was about to tell Deacon that he could not have been further from the truth when she paused. Was it possible? It *was* true that if Mary had indeed been at the cooking school at nine o'clock, she could not have committed the crime at the museum. It was also true that Oona had not cared for Mary's criticism. But the two things were unrelated, as far as she could tell.

"You are wrong, Deacon," Oona said as she peered out the carriage window. "I'm simply after the truth."

She watched the street roll by, hardly noticing the candlestick trees that lined this section of the street, their flickering light pushing back the night. A lone cello played a mournful tune along the sidewalk, devoid of a player.

Farther up the street she saw an owl on a tree branch staring fixedly at the ghostly image of a transparent rat. The rat ran up the tree and jumped to a window ledge. The instant the ghost rat touched the ledge, it lost its balance and fell to the ground and once again climbed the tree where it would leap unsuccessfully for the ledge. Each time the rat climbed the tree, the owl took a swat at it with its thick talon, and each time the talon went right through the transparent rodent. The scene continued on in a seemingly endless loop.

Seeing the ghost made her think of her family. Oona knew that ghosts were real. Many of those buried in the Dark Street Cemetery appeared in their ghostly forms every night. It was only because of an army of poltergeists guarding the entrance that no ghost could exit, nor could any living human enter until daybreak, after the specters returned to their graves. She had often wondered if any of her family members appeared within the cemetery after dark. And sometimes she was not sure if she truly wished to know.

But then again, if she were able to speak with the ghost of her father, she wondered if he would be able to tell her who the Rose Thieves were. Or perhaps, even more importantly, he could tell her how proud of her he was, and how much he loved her. But would he really be proud of her? she wondered. So far she had not discovered anything about the people who had murdered him.

As Oona watched the looping ghost rat disappear in the distance, she let loose a sigh, realizing that in all of the years following the funerals, she had yet to visit her parent's graves.

The carriage pulled to a stop in front of a six-story brick building. The rickety-looking structure leaned so heavily upon its neighboring building that the two appeared in danger of becoming one.

"The Culinary Institute!" Samuligan called.

Oona stepped to the curb, and Deacon flew to her shoulder. To her surprise, Samuligan climbed down from the driver's seat.

"Are you coming with us, Samuligan?" Oona asked.

"I do love cooking," the faerie replied. "I was known as somewhat of a dab hand in the kitchen back in Faerie. But I can always learn something new."

Oona grinned at him. While it was true that Samuligan prepared all of their meals, she had never actually seen him working in the kitchen. She had always assumed he did all the cooking by magic, and the thought of the ominous-looking faerie working over a stove was quite amusing.

"Well, all right...but be on your best behavior," Oona said.

The faerie's expression became one of utmost seriousness, and he crossed his heart with his finger.

"The institute appears to be on the second floor," Deacon said. He gestured with one wing toward a sign beside the front steps.

> 1ST FLOOR: LADY MATILDA'S FLOWER SHOP
> 2ND FLOOR: THE RUDE CULINARY INSTITUTE
> 3RD FLOOR: DARK STREET DANCE ACADEMY

The upper three stories appeared to be filled with apartments.

Oona entered first, ascending the front steps and stepping through the open doorway into an entryway. From there they ascended a spiraling wooden staircase to the second floor, where they came upon a door with the word RUDE written on it in large red letters. Below the red letters, written in a smaller white font, were the words: CULINARY INSTITUTE.

"This is the place," Oona said, and pushed open the door.

"*You're late!*" a man shouted.

Oona was taken aback. She had thought she was paying a surprise visit to the cooking school, but a thin, very large-nosed man in a tall white chef's hat was shouting at her from a nearby table.

The wide room took up the entire second floor and was filled with various tables and cooking stations, many of which were occupied by student chefs. The students wore long white aprons, and Oona recognized Mr. Bop at once. His apron looked to be the size of a large tablecloth. To the right of Mr. Bop's station stood Adler's sister, Isadora Iree. Blonde hair piled artfully upon her head, Isadora looked as pretty as ever, even in her cooking apron, and Oona could not say that she was happy to see her. The two of them, Oona and Isadora, had never been friends.

At the far end of the room, a low stage rose several feet from the floor. Upon the stage stood a table and three chairs. Two of the chairs were occupied. Oona guessed that this was the judge's table. There, sitting in the middle seat, was Mary Shusher, looking quite surprised to see Oona. The young woman's mouth hung slightly open, and Oona was satisfied to see that she was fidgeting nervously in her chair.

The other judge was a bit of a surprise to Oona. Sitting beside Mary was none other than Hector Grimsbee, the blind actor who had applied for the position of Wizard's apprentice over six months ago. As ever, Grimsbee's white eyes, completely devoid of pupils, appeared to stare at her in rather unnerving way.

"Well, what are you just standing there for?" the man in the chef's hat shouted at Oona. His eyes bulged in their sockets. "We are ready to start and we need our final judge!"

Oona's mouth fell open in surprise. "There seems to be some sort of mistake. I'm not—"

The man's face reddened, and his nostrils flared. "Don't tell me you're not late, because the class started three minutes ago and we've been waiting for you. I do not take lightly to lateness in my judges."

Oona threw a hand to her hip. "And who are you?"

"I?" the man said, looking highly offended. "Who am I? Why, I am *Chef* Rude."

"You most certainly are," Deacon said from Oona's shoulder.

The man ignored the raven and spoke directly to Oona. "Take your seat at the judge's table so we can start."

Oona once again opened her mouth to assure the chef that she was not a food judge, but all at once it became clear that this was the perfect opportunity to question Mary Shusher, who was still looking shocked to see Oona there.

"Very good," Oona said, and started toward the judge's table. "Where is the usual third judge?"

"Mr. Vanderbean?" the chef said. "After our last class, he told me he was never coming back. He said I had offended him in some way. Can you imagine?"

"I can, actually," Oona said.

The chef seemed not to have heard her. "I thought for sure he would come back anyway. This is one of the most prestigious culinary schools, not only on Dark Street but in the entire world. But now that you're here, we'll send Vanderbean away if he shows up. He had a weak stomach, you know. Couldn't handle the spice."

"She's not going to judge us, is she?" Isadora Iree asked. "She has no experience judging."

Mary Shusher looked quite nervous, though when she spoke, she sounded genuinely concerned. "Have you any qualifications?"

Oona hopped onto the stage and slid the empty chair out from behind the table. "I *have* tasted food before."

Mary nodded solemnly. "Of course. I didn't mean to suggest that you have no taste. It's just that you must know how to critique the food as well. Tasting is one thing. Expressing that taste requires a certain level of knowledge and skill. It is an art form really."

"The main thing," said Hector Grimsbee in a loud, theatrical voice, "is to smell the food. If it does not smell good, it will not taste good."

"*Silence!*" Chef Rude cried, and all went quiet. Somewhere in the room a faucet could be heard leaking as the chef rounded on Samuligan. "And who are you?"

To Oona's great amusement, Samuligan removed his cowboy hat before reaching inside and pulling out a long white cooking apron. He began enthusiastically tying it around his waist and then stood at attention beside one of the empty cooking stations.

"I," he said in his sly faerie tone, "am Samuligan the Fay...and I am your newest student."

He snapped his fingers, and the sound cracked against the walls like thunder. Everyone jumped. For a moment Chef Rude only stared at the faerie, blinking, and then he seemed to come out of a daze.

"Of course you are," Chef Rude said. He turned to the rest of the class and clapped his hands together. "Tonight we are cooking one of the most difficult dishes known to mankind...the dreaded Chicken Cordon Bleu!"

Several of the students gasped.

"Oh, dear," said Mr. Bop, who used a hand towel to wipe at his forehead.

"What's the matter, Mr. Bop?" Isadora said tauntingly. "Can't handle the heat?"

Mr. Bop slitted his eyes at her but did not respond. Oona frowned. It seemed that Isadora Iree was just as competitive and snooty as ever. Though Oona was a judge and knew she should not have such prejudicial thoughts before even tasting the food, she hoped that Mr. Bop's dish would prove to be superior to Isadora's, especially since Isadora had nearly cheated her way to a victory over Oona in the Magician's Tower Contest.

"You have forty minutes to complete your dish," Chef Rude said. "And the time starts...now!"

The student chefs began running about their cooking stations, pulling pots and pans from beneath counters and utensils from drawers. They scrambled for ingredients along the tall pantry wall, which occupied one whole side of the room. Oona could feel the floor shake as Mr. Bop made his way quickly toward a glass jar full of what looked like bread crumbs, but the enormous man's hand closed down on nothing as the jar shot magically across the room into Samuligan's outstretched fingers.

"What the...?" Mr. Bop said, looking around for the

jar.

"What seems to be the trouble, Mr. Bop?" Chef Rude chided. "You look lost. A chef must never be lost in his own kitchen."

"That's right," Isadora said as she opened a tin of cooking oil to pour into her pan, but like Mr. Bop's bread crumbs, Isadora's pan flew off the counter and into Samuligan's hand. It occurred too quickly for Isadora to understand what was happening, and she poured the oil straight onto the countertop.

"Concentrate on your own work, Miss Iree." Chef Rude scolded her. "A great chef never wastes ingredients."

Isadora shouted when she realized what she was doing and looked wildly around for her pan. She eyed Samuligan suspiciously as he placed the pan atop his wood-burning stove. He flashed his eyes at her, displaying his frightening grin, and Isadora did not dare accuse him.

"Now, that was interesting magic," said Mary Shusher, who had clearly seen everything. "Though it would have been better if he had made some sparks or flashes as well. It would have accentuated his spell work."

Oona's mouth pulled into a tight line, and she clinched her fists. Criticizing Oona's magic was one thing—even if she didn't like it, Oona could reasonably accept that her own skills could use improvement—but that Mary could have the audacity to criticize Samuligan the Fay's magic, good intentions or not, Oona found infuriating.

Mr. Bop, who was now heating a pan over his stove, gave Oona a friendly wave, and she waved back.

"Oh, you mustn't socialize with the contestants," Mary said sweetly to Oona. "It is unprofessional. We must remain impartial and objective."

"Isn't lying unprofessional as well?" Oona asked in a hushed tone.

Mary looked surprised, though Oona suspected it was just an act. "Lying? What do you mean?"

98

Oona turned in her chair. "Tell me, Mary, why did you lie about your whereabouts on Monday night? I have it on good authority that you were not with your grandmother on the night of the theft at the museum, but you were here, working as a food judge...just as you are every Monday and Wednesday night."

Mary turned to face Oona, her eyes all at once like piercing daggers. It was most uncharacteristic of the sweet, helpful exterior she usually portrayed, and Deacon cawed uncomfortably from Oona's shoulder. Oona braced herself for a hard rebuke....

But then Mary's expression fell, and she looked disappointed. "I...I lied because I didn't want my mother to know what I'm doing. As I told you yesterday, she doesn't like my being a critic. Since Adler was there when we were talking, I was afraid that if he knew what I was doing, he might tell my mother...even by accident. If she found out, she would be furious. She is adamant that one day I should become a full-fledged librarian like her."

Deacon cocked his head thoughtfully to one side. "But...if you live with your parents, then how can they not know that you are coming here?"

Mary shrugged. "They have their book club every Monday, Wednesday, and Friday night. They never know I'm gone because I leave just after they do, and get home before. And my grandmother never tells them."

Oona stared at her for a moment, feeling disappointed. "So that's all there is to it? You lied because you didn't want your mother to find out?"

"Or my father," Mary said. "He thinks being a critic is a waste of time. Especially for a woman."

Oona's mouth fell open. "What does being a woman have to do with it?"

"Oh, don't get me wrong. He's not one of these completely chauvinistic men who want women simply to sit quietly and be dutiful. He's just a very practical sort of man, concerned that a woman would never get hired by the newspaper, which is what I want to do." Mary rubbed one hand against her cheek and spoke as if to herself. "But here I am, against his wishes, volunteering as a food critic."

A shock of sympathy penetrated Oona's heart. She knew what it was like to long for the approval of her parents, especially her father, whom she so often aspired to be like. And though her parents were both gone, she could easily imagine what it would be like to feel their disapproval; despite Oona's own misgivings about Mary's opinions, she had to admire the young woman's ingenuity for finding a way to follow her dream, regardless of her parents' wishes.

Oona was almost tempted to tell Mary as much, but she felt too foolish to open her mouth. Mary was, after all, still a person of interest in the case, even if she did have an alibi, and as Mary herself had pointed out, socializing would be unprofessional.

A burst of light caught Oona's eye. Everyone turned to look. Samuligan held two cast iron frying pans, one in each hand, and was presently tossing a burning ball of purplish fire from one pan to the other. Each time the fire hit the pan it would sizzle and hiss. It was quite spectacular to watch, and it took Oona several seconds to realize that within the flame was some sort of thickening sauce.

"Such technique I have never seen before!" exclaimed Chef Rude, apparently transfixed with Samuligan's cooking style. "Brilliant!"

"How's mine looking, Chef Rude?" Isadora asked.

The chef rounded on her, clearly displeased that she should have interrupted him, and then gazed disapprovingly down at the contents of her pan.

"Yours is looking shriveled and slimy," he said.

"Well, it's not done yet," Isadora said, but the chef had already turned to Mr. Bop's station.

"This," he began, and Mr. Bop looked up hopefully, "looks like someone has already eaten it and then spit it back into the pan."

"Well, it's how it tastes that matters," Mr. Bop said, sounding quite hurt.

"Actually, presentation is half of a good meal," Mary Shusher explained to Oona.

"And smell is the other half," Hector Grimsbee said with a dramatic sweep of his arm.

"I suppose that leaves no room for taste then," Oona said.

Mary's well-plucked eyebrows slid closer together. "You aren't going to tell her, are you? My mother?"

Oona considered this for a moment. "I can't see any logical reason to do so."

Mary took Oona's hand and gave it a squeeze. "Oh, thank you, Oona. I will tell them eventually, but only when the time is right."

Oona nodded uncomfortably, pulling her hand away from Mary's surprisingly strong grip. Just then a loud bang echoed around the room. Oona turned to discover Samuligan pulling fistfuls of glittery powder from his pocket and tossing them into the hot pan. Each fistful exploded like gunpowder, sending sparks of blue and white in every direction. The other student chefs were jumping back, attempting to avoid the sparks.

But Chef Rude moved in closer, eyes wide. "Look at how crisp your outer crumb layer is getting, and so fast! It is perfection."

"That's not fair," Isadora said, sounding quite huffy. "He's using magic."

Chef Rude spun on his heels and peered down the sides of his narrow nose at her. "A master chef uses *all* of his skills to create his dish."

"Or *her* dish," Isadora said.

The chef peered once again into her frying pan and sniffed. "If *she* can call such a shriveled morsel a dish."

Isadora's mouth tightened. "I do," she said, though her

voice betrayed her insecurity.

Mr. Bop began to chuckle, but then stopped when Chef Rude turned to his workstation. The chef looked into his pan, picked it up by the handle, and held it beneath Mr. Bop's jiggling jowls. "This is already overdone! I expect better of you, Mr. Bop."

To both Oona's and Mr. Bop's astonishment, the chef tipped the contents of the pan into the garbage.

"Now, start again!" Chef Rude said before striding across the room toward another terrified-looking student.

Mr. Bop stood there for a long moment, looking down into the trash at the contents of his entrée. At last, he seemed to come to himself and returned to the pantry to start again from scratch.

"That was simply rude," Oona said.

"He has to learn somehow," said Mary, once again back to her sweet, informative self. "His food is often overseasoned and much too salty. That ruins the palate, you know."

"The what?" Oona said.

"Palate," Deacon interjected. "Meaning: the roof of the mouth, or sense of taste."

"I think Mr. Bop is an excellent cook," said Hector Grimsbee. "The aromas he creates are divine."

The rest of the forty minutes was whittled away with Chef Rude alternately praising Samuligan for his magical pyrotechnics and berating the rest of the class for their clumsiness and incompetence. Samuligan never once left his pan, but instead would simply snap his fingers and the ingredient he needed would fly from the pantry shelves—or from the hands of a nearby student chef—and into his red-hot cooking skillet. Oona was amazed that his dish was not burned to ash, somehow maintaining a perfectly crispy and quite delicious-looking color.

Soon Oona's mouth began to water.

"Time is up!" the chef called.

Looking tired and bedraggled, the student chefs were all given five minutes to plate their dishes in any artful way they liked, and then asked to line up in front of the judging table. Oona counted eight contestants, including Samuligan, who lined up behind Mr. Bop at the front of the line. Isadora was just behind the faerie, and Oona could see her looking daggers into Samuligan's back.

As hungry as she was, Oona was just beginning to wonder if she would have a large enough appetite to taste each dish, when Mr. Bop presented his entrée before them.

"The presentation is lacking somewhat in originality," said Mary Shusher straightaway. "Though not unappetizing. Much improved from last week, Mr. Bop."

Mr. Bop did not seem to know how to react.

Admittedly, it was not the most elegantly plated dish Oona had ever seen, but she was impressed that Mr. Bop had been able to finish in time, regardless of having to start his meal over again, and it looked delicious.

"It smells edible," said Hector Grimsbee.

The three of them took a piece of the finely breaded chicken and chewed. Oona hadn't realized how hungry she had been, and she swallowed her bite after several chews. Mary, however, continued to chew for what might have been half a minute before swallowing.

"Tough," was all she said.

"Tough?" said Mr. Bop. "Why, I never!"

"No arguing with the judges, Mr Bop!" Chef Rude snapped. "Remember what happened last Monday."

Mr. Bop's mouth clamped shut, and even through his multicolored tattoos Oona could see his face redden.

"I thought it was just right," Hector Grimsbee said, and patted his stomach. "I could smell it all the way down."

Oona cringed at this, and said: "It was delicious, Mr. Bop. I commend you."

She couldn't help but feel slightly guilty about this judgment, however, because she knew that Mary had been right. The chicken had been on the tough side, but Oona liked Mr. Bop too much to say so. It occurred to her that this business of being an impartial critic was harder than she might have thought.

Mr. Bop smiled graciously at her, the tattoos about his face scrunching up at the corners of his mouth. "Why thank you, Miss Crate. I'm pleased that you—"

"Next!" said Chef Rude.

Mr. Bop's mouth once again snapped shut, and he stepped aside to allow Samuligan room to set down his plate. All three judges gasped, staring at the crispy golden chicken before them. The crust appeared to sparkle, as if it had been coated in precious glitter, and the steam that rose from its surface moved like fingers, coaxing the observers closer, encouraging them to taste its playful yet sumptuous texture.

Despite his solid white eyes, Hector Grimsbee seemed hypnotized by the faerie's dish, breathing in slow, deep breaths, lost in the aroma.

"Dig in," Samuligan said.

But at first Oona was afraid even to touch the food, fearful of destroying such a beautifully crafted work of art. And she did not seem to be the only one. Both Grimsbee and Mary appeared to hesitate, as if to bask for as long as possible in the presence of the plate...but at last Oona reached forward with her fork, and the other judges did the same. They took their bites at the same time, and then simultaneously burst into tears.

Oona could not remember ever having tasted something so succulent. So divine. So...

"Perfect!" said Mary, who was practically bawling over her plate.

Oona knew exactly what she was speaking of. It *was* perfection in a single bite, and she wept because she knew that never again would she taste something so pure, so perfectly true. In that single taste was all the sorrows of the world, and all the joys, and all the dreams, and hopes, and despair. It was all there. All of it. More than Oona had thought possible. Her heart seemed to grow heavy and yet float at the same time. She felt infinite.

And then it was over. She swallowed and wiped her face with a napkin.

"This is the clear winner," Mary Shusher said, her voice trembling with emotion.

"The undeniable winner," agreed Hector Grimsbee, whose tear-streaked face had more color in it than Oona had ever seen before.

"Samuligan, you won!" Oona exclaimed.

In a grand sweeping gesture, the faerie removed his hat and took a bow, clearly pleased with himself.

"Wait a minute!" Isadora shouted. "You haven't tasted the rest of ours. You have to taste *all* of our dishes before you declare a winner. That's the rule!"

Mary sighed and looked at Chef Rude.

"It is the rule," the chef said with a shrug, and he pulled a fork from his pocket to taste Samuligan's dish for himself. As expected, the chef burst into tears of utter joy.

"Very well," said Mary, who did not seem pleased at all to have to taste anything else after having tasted such perfection, and beckoned Isadora forward.

Isadora placed her dish before them, and as she did so, Oona's heart leapt into her throat. She gasped, shaking her head as if she were not seeing right.

Isadora's plating technique was beautiful; the way the entrée sat just off center but was balanced by an artful display of sauce liberally dribbled around the plate's edge. But it was neither the sauce nor the chicken that inspired Oona's reaction. It was the thin red ribbon that Isadora had used as decoration on top of the chicken that caused Oona to lose her breath. More specifically, it was the knot that Isadora had chosen to use. Not just any knot. It was *the* knot. The one Oona had been searching for.

It was the Rose Knot.

"Oh, dear," said Mary Shusher, picking up the knotted ribbon between her thumb and pointer finger. "I'm afraid that inedible garnish is a real no-no. The reason for this is that someone might try to eat it, and then—"

"Shush, Mary!" Oona said forcefully, and then turned to Isadora. "Where did you learn to tie this knot?"

Isadora looked as if she were confused. But Oona's heart was thrumming. She did not think that Isadora Iree was one of the Rose Thieves—she was too young—but whoever had taught that knot to Isadora just might be a suspect, not only for stealing the Faerie Carbuncle, but also for the murder of Oona's father.

Isadora shook her head and shrugged. "I found it in a book."

"A book?" Oona asked urgently. "What book?"

"A book I checked out of the library," Isadora said. "But I've already turned it back in."

Oona jumped to her feet. "The public library? What was it called? What section was it in?"

Isadora's eyebrows rose in surprise. "Why, just look at it," she said, pointing at the knot, which was still being held between Mary Shusher's fingers. "It is a work of art. Where else would I have found it but in the art section?"

Chapter Eight

The Art of
Abraham McGillicuddy

The following morning Oona was awake and waiting at the museum front entrance before nine o'clock, Deacon on her shoulder. Her plan was to get an early start on finding the art book Isadora had returned to the library and still have time to attend the political rally that afternoon.

At ten till nine, Mrs. Shusher, the librarian, and her daughter, Mary, walked up the stone steps and stopped in front of the large wooden door. Mary gave Oona a nervous look, as if afraid that Oona might tell her mother about Mary's secret life as a food critic.

The librarian raised an eyebrow at Oona and said: "I'm afraid, my dear, that Adler Iree is not in today. He has a test at the Magicians Legal Alliance, and so he has the day off from the library."

"Oh, I see," Oona said, her face going quite red. "I'm here to do research, actually."

The librarian gave Oona a skeptical look and was just about to say something when the daytime guard opened the door.

"Hello, Mrs. Shusher," he said.

"Good morning, Victor," she replied and stepped over the threshold into the museum. Mary gave Oona a fleeting glance and followed her mother inside.

When Oona started to follow them in, the guard put up a hand to stop her. "Sorry, but the museum and the library open at nine o'clock. You'll have to wait outside for a few minutes."

"Oh, I see," Oona said, but as the guard began to close the door, she added: "What time do you change shifts from the night shift to the day shift?"

The guard peered at her for a long moment. "No offense intended, miss, but Inspector White told me you'd probably be back, asking more questions. And he said I don't need to answer any of 'em."

Oona shrugged, as if it did not matter. "Yes, of course he did. Inspector White thinks you can't decide for yourself who to talk to."

"Huh?"

"And maybe he's right not to trust you. Maybe you're a suspect, and he thinks that you'll accidentally let something slip to me...and I will solve the case before him."

The guard frowned. "Me, a suspect? But I'm the one who found Elbert tied up. I cut him loose. Why would I have anything to do with it?"

"Elbert?" Oona asked. "That's the night watchman's name?" She had a vague recollection of the guard having told her this before.

"That's right," the guard said. He sounded indignant. "Elbert Hackelsmith. And I don't care what the inspector thinks, I've got nothing to hide."

"Of course you don't," Oona said. "Now what time did you say you usually switch from the night shift to the day shift?"

This time the guard did not hesitate. "Seven o'clock every morning."

"And that's what time you found the night watchman, Elbert Hackelsmith, on Tuesday morning?"

"That's right," said Victor the guard. "Found him lying there on the floor all tied up. Mr. Glump, the curator, came in a few minutes later. Told me to fetch the police, so I did, lickety-split. Took the constables nearly two hours to find what was missing."

"The Faerie Carbuncle," Oona said. Again she experienced that uneasy feeling at the thought of the potential power the magical gemstone could bestow its owner. She reminded herself that the spell to activate it was long lost, but still, this did not make her feel much better.

"Yeah. The glass case was broken and everything," said Victor. "The thieves didn't take anything else."

Oona looked past the guard, trying to get a look at the clock in the entryway. "Is it time to open?"

The guard turned. "Oh, look there. So it is."

He stepped aside and let Oona inside.

"Thank you, Victor," she said, and headed upstairs toward the library.

The guard watched her go, shaking his head as if realizing that she had just tricked him into giving her information he had not intended on giving.

"I never was a suspect, was I?" he called after her.

"How should I know?" Oona said. "Inspector White is quite good at accusing innocent people."

She glanced back to see the guard's expression turn from irritation back to concern.

"That was clever of you," Deacon said as they ascended the steps. "Yet I don't see the significance of it. What does it tell us?"

"I don't know," Oona said. "But it's good information to have. It gives us a time frame. The victim, Mr. Elbert Hackelsmith, was attacked at around nine o'clock in the evening and then found at seven o'clock the next morning." Again she thought of how the name Hackelsmith was somehow familiar. "By the way, what do we know about the night watchman?"

Deacon paused, as if searching for the correct data. After a moment he said: "According to the *Dark Street Who's Who*, Elbert Hackelsmith is the night watchman for the Museum of Magical History and has been for nearly ten years. It is his only job on record. He is single and lives alone. He is the son of Wendell and Wanda Hackelsmith, both prominent undertakers."

Oona pushed through the library door. "What else?"

"Nothing factual. There is a rumor that his parents, the Hackelsmiths, were vampires. But this is unproven, and likely something people say because the Hackelsmiths worked with the dead for a living." Deacon began to chuckle, as if he had just made an amusing joke.

Oona gave him a disapproving glance, and then all at once it came to her...where she had heard that name before. Of course, the Hackelsmiths had been the undertakers who had handled the funeral arrangements not only for Oona's father but also for her mother and baby sister.

She came to a sudden halt, thinking how small the world of Dark Street was.

"Are you lost?" came a familiar voice. It was Mary Shusher, who was pushing a cart full of books toward the far end of the room.

"Oh no," Oona said, but then, reconsidering, she added: "Actually, yes. Can you point me in the direction of the art section?"

Mary pointed toward a wall of books close to the reference desk and then came to a stop. She looked as if she were about to say something. She considered Oona for a moment and then in a hushed tone said: "Thank you for not telling my mother about my secret. Maybe one day she will understand." She gestured toward the cart full of books. "But until then, it's a life of shelving books, I'm afraid. By the way, now that I've had time really to think about it, that food your faerie served us last night...I know I ate it, and loved it, but I can't actually seem to remember doing so. It's like I ate it in a dream. Isn't that strange?"

Oona nodded. "You know, I had a similar feeling this morning. I figured it must have been the faerie ingredients and magical technique that somehow wiped it clean from my memory. I asked Samuligan about it, and he said he did it on purpose...to be kind."

"Kind?" asked Mary, clearly perplexed.

Oona had had the same reaction earlier that morning.

Yes, kind, Samuligan had said. *If I had not done so, then every meal from this time forward would be compared to that one...and no meal would ever be able to compete. You might have even stopped eating all together because all other food would seem boring, dull, and gray. By adding an ingredient of forgetfulness, your next meal will now be judged on its own merit...as it should be.*

Oona had marveled at this, astonished that the faerie had had such forethought. Samuligan was truly a master of magic.

But when Oona recounted the conversation to Mary, the assistant librarian frowned at the cart of books. "Yes...or perhaps the meal was not as good as I thought it was. I just don't know." She shook her head in earnest confusion. "Well, I really should get back to work. Good day."

The two of them parted company, Mary rolling her cart in one direction and Oona and Deacon venturing in the other. The art section turned out to be one of the largest sections in the library. The two of them began scanning the shelves for the name of the book Isadora had told Oona about the previous night. Because of the alphabetical system of organization, Oona found the book in no time.

"This is it," she said excitedly and hurried to a nearby table. She set the book down and stared for a moment at the cloth cover: *Knots: The Art of Abraham McGillicuddy.*

Opening to a random page, she discovered a full-page

illustration of one of the most unusual knots she had ever seen. It looked like a dog's head, with long droopy ears and sad eyes. She was not surprised to read that the name of this particular knot was the Sad Dog Knot. The opposite page displayed several much smaller illustrations that showed the various steps that were needed in order to achieve the knot using a single piece of rope. Tiny arrows showed which end of the rope slipped into which loop.

"Extraordinary," Deacon said from her shoulder. He leaned forward to get a better look.

"*Quite* extraordinary," Oona said. "I've never seen anything like it."

She turned the page to find an equally fascinating knot known as the Pharaoh's Pyramid, in which the rope formed a perfect four-sided pyramid. The slim book was filled with page after page of unusual knots, all of which were dazzling to the eye even in the illustrations. Oona could only imagine that they would be even more spectacular when actually tied in a piece of rope.

And then she found it, the page containing the Rose Knot. There it was, illustrated in its complex glory. Deacon let out a short gasp, and Oona placed a hand to her mouth. She found the image to be wondrous and yet ominous at the same time. The knot was so complicated that the instructional illustrations filled not only the entire neighboring page, but took up the two following pages as well.

Oona was impressed that Isadora had been able to accomplish it the previous night. It started her thinking. "You know, Deacon, if this book was part of the public library's collection, then anyone would have been able to check it out. Anyone could have learned to tie these knots."

"Look in the front to see who else has checked it out," Deacon suggested.

Oona did so. A card had been stuck to the inside front cover with the words PROPERTY OF DARK STREET PUBLIC LIBRARY printed at the top. Below this were lines where anyone who had checked the book out would need to sign their name. There was only one name: Isadora Iree.

Oona ran a hand through her long black hair, shaking her head. "It seems that Isadora is the only one who has ever checked this book out. And the date is from last week. But look at how old this book appears to be. Strange that no one has ever checked it out before."

"Perhaps it is newly acquired," Deacon reasoned.

Just then, Mary Shusher was returning to the reference desk with her cart. Oona carried the book to the counter and opened it to the inside cover. She pointed to the card.

"I was wondering, Mary, if Isadora Iree is really the only person who has ever checked this book out?"

Mary glanced at the card but was already shaking her head. "Not likely. That is part of a very old collection of art books. In fact, I know I have shelved it before, back at the old library."

Oona tapped her finger on Isadora's name. "Then how come she is the only one who signed it out?"

"Because those cards are new," Mary said. "We got rid of the old cards when we moved to the new library because my mother wanted to start the system over fresh. Every book got a new card."

"Oh," Oona said, shoulders sinking slightly, but then all at once she brightened. "Do you remember who checked it out from the old library?"

Mary shook her head. "It was a long time ago. I'm sorry."

Oona nodded. "Well, would you mind checking it out to me? I should like to take it home."

Mary removed the name card from the front of the book and handed Oona a fountain pen.

"Sign your name here."

Oona did so, and Mary dropped the card into a file box before placing another card into the book, this one printed with the due date.

Oona thanked Mary and headed toward the exit. With the book tucked beneath one arm, Oona pushed through the library door and nearly ran right into Mary's father on the steps that led down to the museum.

"Ho-ho! Watch where you're going there, miss!" Mr. Shusher said.

The two of them did a little dance, trying to get around each other.

Perhaps it was because Oona was so frustrated with not finding any real clue as to who the thieves were that she couldn't stop herself from blurting out: "What is it that you are hiding, Mr. Shusher?"

Mr. Shusher came to an abrupt halt. "I beg your pardon?"

His highly lined face scowled, and his eyes squinted at her from beneath the brim of his bowler hat.

"Be careful," Deacon whispered in her ear.

Oona ignored him. "Yesterday, Mr. Shusher, I overheard you say to your wife that you had hidden something. What was it?"

Mr. Shusher continued to stare at her for a long moment, his face a mask of anger. Finally, he stepped toward her and began cracking his knuckles. Oona could not tell if it was just a nervous habit of his, or if he was trying to be threatening. Either way, it was quite unnerving.

Oona moved against the stair railing, and Deacon puffed up his chest menacingly on her shoulder.

Mr. Shusher jabbed his finger at her. "You mind your own business."

Oona held the knot book up in front of her like a shield. Mr. Shusher's eyes flicked briefly toward the cover, and then as if realizing what he was doing, he shook his head and turned his back on her, disappearing through the library door. Oona let out a quick breath and placed her hand on the rail to steady herself.

"That was reckless," Deacon said. He shook his

feathers as he shrank back to his normal size. "What possessed you to confront him like that? He might be one of the Rose Thieves, for all we know."

Oona was nodding. She started back down the stairs. "Mr. Shusher and his wife certainly have had access to this book. Who knows the library's collection better than the librarian? Do you think he recognized the book when I held it up?"

Deacon shook his head. "I have no idea."

Oona's mouth twisted to one side. "I couldn't tell, either. It happened too fast."

Deacon looked thoughtful. "But then again, they both have alibis for the night of the theft."

Oona pushed through the museum door and squinted against the outside glare. "They *supposedly* have alibis, but we can't be certain. After all, Mary had a supposed alibi, but she lied, didn't she?"

"You think the mother and father are lying as well?"

"It is a possibility. We should find out more about this book club of theirs, and see if the Shushers were, in fact, in attendance the night of the theft."

Deacon clacked his beak several times. "Might I suggest you spend at least *some* time researching your next battle test?"

"What, you don't think I have done fine so far?" Oona asked.

"You have done quite well, according to your uncle...but it couldn't hurt."

Oona stopped at the curb and looked up at Samuligan, who was waiting patiently atop the carriage. He looked as if he were lost in some sort of trance. His dark eyes did not appear to be focusing on anything in particular, yet there was a slight curving about his mouth, a mischievous bend, and Oona couldn't help but wonder if the faerie were preparing for the challenge later that day. It made her shiver to look at him.

"Perhaps you are right, Deacon," Oona half whispered. "If Samuligan is preparing for this challenge, I might want to do the same." And then in a louder voice, which seemed to snap Samuligan out of his daze, she said: "But first we must pick up Uncle Alexander and Mrs. Carlyle. We have a campaign rally to attend."

Chapter Nine

The Rally

"Let me guess," said Mrs. Carlyle. "That's him there. The one in the top hat."

Oona, Deacon, the Wizard, and Mrs. Carlyle approached the crowd of people surrounding the stage. Samuligan, who seemed uninterested in human politics, had stayed behind with the horse and carriage.

The sun was out, lighting up the park grounds like green carpet, turning the shade beneath the trees into welcoming shelter.

Mrs. Carlyle pointed toward the growing crowd, but Oona knew precisely whom the maid was referring to. Oona had spotted Adler's shabby top hat and ragged cloak from as far away as the park entrance. He stood near the edge of the crowd beside his sister, Isadora, and their mother, Madame Iree, the famous dressmaker.

"Perhaps you'll give us an introduction," the maid said.

Oona's face went very warm.

She was impressed by the number of people in attendance. There must have been at least three hundred people.

"Looks like a good turnout," said the Wizard.

"Indeed," Mrs. Carlyle agreed.

"She'll need more votes than this to win though, don't you think?" Oona asked.

"She will indeed," Deacon said. "But look at that fancy display. Must have cost a fortune."

Deacon was referring to the festive decorations that had been hung from the trees and draped around the stage. Molly Morgana Moon's campaign staff had been hard at work since Oona had last seen the stage the day before. Signs hung from every tree limb, each of them displaying a printed photograph of the candidate's smiling face.

The image accentuated Molly Morgana Moon's large eyes, which looked both concerned and likable at the same time. Above her image had been printed slogans such as A VOTE FOR ME IS A VOTE FOR YOU! and LET'S TAKE BACK OUR STREET!

It was all very professional and quite expensive-looking.

"Molly Morgana Moon has always been good at raising money," The Wizard said. "She knows all the right people. Perhaps I was wrong, and she does stand a chance after all."

That was encouraging, Oona thought, and then came to a stop at the edge of the crowd right behind Adler. She tapped him on the shoulder.

"Ah, Miss Crate," he said, spinning around and tipping his hat.

"Hello, Adler," Oona said. "I believe you know my uncle, the Wizard."

Adler bowed slightly. "Of course. Good day to you, sir."

"And a fine day it is," the Wizard said agreeably.

"And this is Mrs. Carlyle, our new housemaid," Oona said.

Adler's eyebrows rose slightly at being introduced to a

housemaid, which was highly unusual, Oona knew, but he recovered quickly and tipped his hat. "A pleasure to meet you, Mrs. Carlyle."

"The pleasure is mine, Mr. Iree," Mrs. Carlyle said, and gave Oona an overt wink. "And don't you think Miss Crate is looking lovely today?"

Adler gave a half shrug before answering: "She does...but then again, she looks lovely every day."

"Really? Is that so?" said a sharp, disbelieving voice, and Oona turned to discover Isadora staring at her, arms crossed.

"Hello, Isadora," Oona said. "How are you today?"

Isadora glanced around, ignoring the question. "Where is your faerie servant? Off gloating over his win from last night?"

Oona almost laughed at the absurdity of this. She had never seen Samuligan gloat in her life. He might be self-assured and unpredictable, but gloating he was not. She decided to give Isadora a taste of her own medicine and ignored the question.

"Where is Roderick Rutherford, Isadora?" Oona asked.

She was speaking of Isadora's overly gallant boyfriend who had helped Isadora cheat her way through the Magician's Tower Contest.

Isadora rolled her eyes. "Oh, him? We broke up last month. Or, I should say, *I* broke up with *him*. He kept going on and on about being chivalrous. Wouldn't shut up about it. He kept wanting to open carriage doors for me and escort me across the street."

Oona's eyebrows shot up in surprise. "But I thought you liked all that, Isadora."

"I do...or, that is to say, I did, until I realized that he did not believe I could do these things for myself. He thought I was incapable. So I dumped him, and that is when mother and I joined the Molly Morgana Moon campaign. You remember my mother, don't you?"

Oona had, of course, met Madame Iree on several occasions. She nodded hello to the dressmaker just as the crowd erupted into applause. The woman whose face was plastered everywhere stepped onto the stage, along with a bearded man who wore a top hat and monocle.

Molly Morgana Moon was a short, immensely attractive woman in her mid-forties. She wore an expensive-looking corseted blue dress with a matching hat that gave her an important air. The dress was tailor-made to fit her short stature, and Oona had an idea that the dress was a Madame Iree original that would not have come cheap.

Oona's heart seemed to swell in her chest as the woman approached the front of the stage and waved to the crowd. It was all so exciting. Molly Morgana Moon was at the forefront not only of women's equality but also of change on Dark Street, and Oona felt excited just to be there, to be a part of it. Though she would not be able to vote until her twenty-first birthday, she still wished for her voice to be heard, and she soon began to cheer along with the rest of the crowd.

"Thank you all for coming," Molly Morgana Moon shouted over the applause. She made a motion for the crowd to quiet down, but the spectators were too excited. Their cheers grew only louder. Mrs. Moon continued to smile as she cast a look at the man in the top hat. He smiled back, as if the reception was just as pleasing to him as it was to her.

"Who is that?" Oona asked, turning to Mrs. Carlyle.

"The gentleman standing beside her?" asked Mrs. Carlyle. "That's her husband."

Deacon said: "Mr. John David Moon. He was the owner of a stock trading company that went belly up a few years ago: Moon Investments. I'm afraid they have fallen into hard times."

Oona looked at the couple's fine attire and almost regal air, and said: "They appear to have recovered quite nicely."

"Appearances can be deceptive," Deacon said. "You of all people should know that."

Oona frowned. "Well, then, where did they get the money for all of this?" She gestured toward the stage and its impressive decorations.

"It's a good question," Deacon said.

At last the spectators began to quiet down, and Molly Morgana Moon could be heard over the crowd. "Thank you all for coming. Thank you so very much. It is an honor to be here."

As the crowd quieted, Oona noticed a short balding man near the side of the stage. He was waving his hands in the air, as if trying to get Mrs. Moon's attention. She didn't appear to notice him, but her husband, John David Moon, did. The smile on John David's face dropped abruptly away as he walked to the side of the stage.

While it seemed everyone in the crowd had eyes only for Molly Morgana Moon, who began her speech by thanking various members of the community for their support, Oona was too distracted by the man at the side of the stage to listen properly. She happened to be on the same side of the stage as he was, and she could see the expression of irritation on John David Moon's face as he knelt to speak with him. They spoke in whispers—too soft for anyone to hear—but from where Oona stood, it was quite clear that the two of them were arguing.

Mr. Moon shook his head, pointing his finger threateningly at the balding man. Oona watched the two of them curiously as the exchange grew even more heated. Oona was contemplating moving closer so that she might hear what the two of them were arguing about when a second distraction pulled her attention toward the park entrance.

A group of thirty or more rather loud latecomers came clomping across the park, the majority of them holding handmade signs over their heads. It wasn't until they got a bit closer that Oona was able to read them.

Most of the signs exclaimed FINK FOR COUNCIL! or some such variation, though mixed in were an abundance of much ruder signs that said things like WOMEN, STAY IN YOUR PLACE! and DON'T VOTE FOR THE SKIRTS!

Oona took in a startled gasp as she saw the expressions on the faces of the men holding the signs. They were full of hatred and rage. Those who did not carry signs were carrying crudely made clubs.

"Oh, dear," said Deacon.

Mrs. Carlyle took in a sharp breath. "Great Oswald, there's going to be a riot!"

At the mention of the word *riot* many of the spectators on Oona's side of the stage turned to see the approaching mob.

"What's that about?" Adler asked.

"We should all remain calm," the Wizard said.

Surprisingly, it was the word *calm* more so than the word *riot* that caused the nearby spectators to react.

"They've got clubs!" someone cried.

"Run!" shouted another.

A handful of spectators did just that, bolting for the far end of the park, which seemed to be the cue for the mob of angry men to run straight at the crowd.

"But there are women and children in there!" Oona said, shocked at seeing the oncoming wave of swinging clubs and fists.

"I believe that's the point," said the Wizard, who took hold of Oona and pulled her to him.

"We have to do something," Oona said. "People are going to get hurt...or worse."

She could see Molly Morgana Moon beginning to look around from atop the stage to see what the disturbance was. More people from the crowd were beginning to run now, and the mob was nearly on them.

Screams of fright mingled with the belligerent shouts

of the club-wielding men.

"Do you have your wand, Oona?" the Wizard asked urgently.

Oona's hand shot into her dress pocket and pulled out her father's magnifying class.

"Very good. Hexingjer's Barrier should do the trick," the Wizard said, pulling out his own wand and aiming it at the space between the approaching mob and the scattering crowd. "On the count of three."

There was no time to question. She aimed her wand and counted down in rapid succession with her uncle. "One, two, *Bar isth tho!*"

A stream of white wind shot from the ends of both the Wizard's wand and Oona's magnifying glass handle. It swirled thickly like a winter storm before freezing solid, forming a seven-foot wall of ice. Unable to stop their momentum, the approaching hoard of men collided against the wall in a heap of signs and clubs. Several of the men began to throw punches at one another while others picked themselves shakily up from the ground and looked for a way around the wall.

The wall of ice stopped at the edge of the stage, where the more crafty members of the mob now turned their attention.

"They're going to tear it down," Oona said, unsure of how she knew this but certain all the same. "We've got to get Molly Morgana Moon to safety."

As the mob approached the edge of the stage, Oona could see that the balding man was nowhere to be seen, and that John David Moon was taking his wife by the hand and leading her toward the far end of the stage. They had just reached the edge when the entire stage gave a shutter and began to lean sideways.

At least seven strong men were at the other end of the stage heaving with all of their might. Once again the stage shuttered, and then pitched left, tossing Molly Morgana

Moon and her husband into the air.

"*Desendium*," Oona cried, and another windlike spell shot from the end of her wand, over the heads of the scattering crowd, and caught the falling couple just in time, cushioning their fall. They stumbled slightly, and then continued running along with the rest of the crowd toward the second gate entrance at the far end of the park.

Behind them the entire stage collapsed with a resounding crash of metal and wood.

"I believe we have sufficiently deterred them," Uncle Alexander said, peering through the icy wall at the belligerent men on the other side. "And I think no one was hurt. I believe we should be off ourselves, before they figure out they can walk around the end of the wall."

Several members of the mob made as if to scale the wall of ice, but none seemed capable of the climb. Most, however, seemed satisfied with the destruction of the stage and settled on shouting rude names after the fleeing crowd.

Oona felt a hand clamp onto hers and looked around to find Adler Iree standing beside her. In all of the confusion she had forgotten he was there.

"Are your mother and sister all right?" Oona asked.

"They took off that way." He pointed toward the retreating spectators. Without a hint of humor he added: "Don't think I've ever seen Isadora run so fast."

Oona glanced hurriedly around. "Where's Mrs. Carlyle?"

"I believe she made her exit with the others," said the Wizard. "As we would be wise to do ourselves." He grabbed Oona's other hand and led them in the direction of the northernmost park gate.

Oona and Adler said their good-byes outside the park gate, where he departed with his sister and Madame Iree. Oona looked all around the cluster of chattering pedestrians for any sign of Mrs. Carlyle, but the maid was nowhere to be seen.

"She is probably halfway back to Pendulum House," Samuligan said when Oona inquired if he had seen the maid. He sat atop the carriage in the driver's seat and pointed up the street, his mouth curving into an amused smirk. "I saw her heading north for safety, along with all those other panicking people."

Oona opened her mouth to admonish the faerie for finding humor in the chaos and hysteria, but in that instant someone bumped into her and she staggered into the carriage wheel. Deacon cawed from her shoulder.

"Oh, dear, I'm so sorry," said a voice, and Oona turned to discover none other than Molly Morgana Moon standing before her and extending a hand. "Please excuse me. I'm a bit shaken from...from..."

Oona took the woman's hand and straightened. "No need to explain. We were there. We saw it all happen."

Molly Morgana Moon's eyes—which at first had appeared quite dazed—seemed to come into sharp focus on Oona's face. "I know who you are. You are Oona Crate, the Wizard's apprentice." She looked to the Wizard, who stood to Oona's right. "Alexander. My goodness, it's been years."

The Wizard gave a slight bow. "Too many, Molly."

She turned back to Oona and smiled. "I knew your mother."

"You did?" Oona asked, surprised. She stared into Mrs. Moon's face, feeling quite in awe. Here, standing before her, was a woman she greatly admired. A woman who was brave enough to do what no other woman before her had attempted to do: run for political office on Dark Street. The knowledge that she was an acquaintance of Oona's mother was bittersweet to say the least.

"I did, indeed," Molly Morgana Moon said. "Octavia and I went to school together at the Academy of Fine Young Ladies, and years later we worked together to gain the right for women to vote here on Dark Street. You know, I always wondered if it would be she who one day ran for office...but alas, that was not meant to be." She sighed, looking momentarily lost in memory.

Oona opened and closed her mouth, unsure of how to respond. She fidgeted awkwardly with the sleeve of her dress.

Molly Morgana Moon's eyes once more seemed to focus on Oona, and she took in a sharp breath as if she only just realized what she had said. "Oh, my dear...I didn't mean..."

"It's all right," Oona quickly lied, and then, looking for a way to change the subject, she boldly brushed at a spot of dirt on the front of Mrs. Moon's dress.

"Oh, look at that," Molly Morgana Moon said, and then looked around. She caught the eye of her husband, who stood nearby, clearly on the lookout for more trouble. She turned back to Oona. "What a tragic outcome. I would say I'm happy you came, but..." She gestured toward the iron bars of the park, through which could be seen the tumbled remains of the stage. "I might say that an anti-demonstration was to be expected...but I—we—did not expect such violence." She frowned. "And no sign of the police to do anything about it."

"Does that surprise you?" the Wizard asked.

Mrs. Moon shook her head. "Sadly, no. There are not enough constables to cover thirteen miles of street, and that nincompoop Inspector White is good for nothing. All those men should be arrested, but not one of them will be caught." She paused a moment, peering toward the far end of the park.

"Did you do that, Alexander?"

She pointed toward the wall of ice in the distance. Most of the men who had attacked the rally were already gone, and the wall was now beginning to melt in the warm sunlight.

"I did," said the Wizard. "Along with Oona. It was she who cushioned your fall from the collapsing stage with a brilliant bit of spell work that I myself did not think fast enough to attempt."

Mrs. Moon's face seemed to light up as she looked directly into Oona's large green eyes. She was not a tall woman, only an inch or so taller than Oona, but her presence was extraordinary.

"So, I have you to thank for that, do I? I was wondering why we managed to keep on our feet after being thrown so forcefully. What a remarkable young woman you are."

Oona's face reddened. "Why do you think those men attacked like they did?"

Molly Morgana Moon's expression hardened. "It was my rival, Tobias Fink—I'm sure of it. I saw some of the men carrying his campaign signs. He likely gave them cash."

"Cash from Red Martin," Oona said.

Mrs. Moon looked surprised but then began to nod. "Yes, you would know about Red Martin from your father. He would have spoken about him."

Oona nodded, though she did not add that she herself had come face-to-face with Red Martin on several occasions.

"That was some display you put up," the Wizard said. "Must have cost a pretty penny."

Oona looked at her uncle in surprise. Talking of money was something he rarely did.

Mrs. Moon's husband, John David, suddenly stepped forward, looking highly offended. "I hope, Alexander, that you are not implying that we have been taking money from the likes of Red Martin!"

The Wizard spread his hands in front of him. "I meant nothing of the sort. I was merely stating what a shame it was to have all been for nothing."

"Yes, well, that's the price of politics!" Mr. Moon said harshly, and then turned to his wife. "Come, Molly. We should get you home."

"Of course, dear," Mrs. Moon said, and then, leaning toward Oona, she whispered in her ear. "Don't mind him. He's just upset at the loss. But we won't let this little setback stop us. In fact, I feel even more determined than ever to crack down on crime." Straightening up again, she extended her hand to Oona, and the two of them shook. "It was a pleasure meeting you, Oona. You remind me a bit of your mother. I hope that I'll see you again, and that you'll continue to give your support. Oh, and thank you again for saving all of our necks. Really, both of you."

And with that, the couple made their way to their carriage and were off, leaving Oona with a feeling of excitement and perplexity all at the same time.

"Come, Oona," said the Wizard. "We should be off ourselves. We have a battle test to prepare for."

Chapter Ten

The Third Test

"Hello, Mrs. Carlyle," Oona said as she and Deacon entered the Pendulum House library. "I was afraid you might have been injured in the riot. Are you quite all right?"

They found the maid busily dusting one of the tree-branch bookshelves in the forest of books.

"Oh, hello, Miss Crate," she said. "Yes, I'm fine. Quite a nasty bit of business that was back there at the park. I thought we were all done for. I'm sorry you had to see it...but that's what we're up against. Better get used to it, if you're going to fight for women's rights. Got to stand our ground, we do."

"Is that why you ran all the way back here?" Deacon asked from Oona's shoulder.

"Deacon!" Oona snapped. "There's no need to be rude."

Deacon looked abashed. "I...I'm sorry, Mrs. Carlyle. I did not mean to cause offense. It's just that...well, you spoke of taking a stand—"

"But I ran for my life," Mrs. Carlyle said. She nodded understandingly.

"Sorry," Oona said. "Deacon can be a bit literal at

times."

"Hmm!" Deacon intoned, and now it was he who sounded offended.

"No, no. It's all right," Mrs. Carlyle said, and Oona could see her cheeks flush pink. "He's right. I did run, just like everyone else. I didn't see any sense in my getting my head cracked open by one of those thug's clubs. And when I talk of taking a stand, I don't necessarily mean physically. Of course, those men were three times as big as me, with clubs and glass bottles. They might be stronger here..." She pointed to her arm. "But not necessarily stronger here..." She pointed to her head. "It's too bad you didn't get to hear Molly Morgana Moon speak today, because she exemplifies just what it means to fight without fists."

"I just met her," Oona said.

"Did you now?" Mrs. Carlyle said wonderingly. "Never have, myself. But I've been a supporter from the get-go."

"Uncle Alexander seems to know her from years ago," Oona said. "Apparently, she and my mother were friends."

"Well, isn't that something," Mrs. Carlyle said earnestly. "Speaking of your uncle, is he all right, too? I saw that bit of magic you two performed just before I turned and ran. I hope he's okay."

"He's fine. I just left him and Samuligan in the entryway."

Mrs. Carlyle glanced around suspiciously.

"Oh, don't worry," Oona said. "Samuligan isn't here. He disappeared as soon as we entered the house. Most likely preparing for my next battle test."

This news did not seem to appease Mrs. Carlyle, who continued to look nervously around.

"The test is to take place in the front gardens," Deacon said in a clear attempt to settle the maid's nerves.

Oona furrowed her brow. "I meant to ask him to help me find a book on the battle tests so that I might prepare as well, but he disappeared before I could do so...and now he doesn't respond to my calling him."

Deacon adjusted his position on her shoulder. "How convenient."

"Precisely," Oona said. "He doesn't want to give me any advantage."

"Well, that's not very gentlemanly," said Mrs. Carlyle.

"Samuligan isn't really a gentleman," Oona said.

"I should say not," said the maid, and then, with a twinkle in her eye, she added: "But speaking of gentlemen, that young Mr. Iree is quite the catch."

"You think so?" Oona asked brightly.

Deacon cawed his disapproval. "Come now. Let's see if we can't find a book in here that will give you a hint of what to expect for this third battle test."

Oona peered around the forest of books and began to shake her head. "Good luck finding anything in here without Samuligan's help."

"Don't you know of any spell that might locate the book you want?" Deacon asked.

Oona considered this. She did not know offhand of any spell that would do the trick, especially since she didn't even know the name of the book they were looking for. But all at once an idea came to her.

"Perhaps I do know a spell," she said, though it was not specifically a spell that was used to find things.

"Well, it must be worth a shot," Deacon said.

Oona thought of the words she had recited yesterday in the park: the spell that would connect her own magic with the magic of the house. The thought of doing the spell without the Wizard made her nervous, but she had a feeling she would be able to do it all the same.

With a deep breath to steady her nerves, she uttered: *"Profundus magicus."*

And just like that, she was plugged in. The house's magic filled her up like warm water, and she knew what she needed to do. She concentrated on her desire: a book containing information on the battle tests.

She snapped her fingers and the sound was like cannon fire. Deacon was startled from her shoulder and Mrs. Carlyle dropped her feather duster, but Oona hardly noticed these things. Her gaze narrowed in on the large book that presently slid out from one of the knottier oaks near the swamp. It hovered off the shelf and then shot across the room straight into Oona's hands.

"Look out!" Deacon shouted, as it seemed the book was moving too fast.

Oona did not so much as wobble as she caught the massive volume and then turned to set the book on top of a table. The words *Apprenticeship Magica* were embossed upon its dark leathery cover, barely legible to the eye. Oona waved her hand over the cover, and the book opened to the exact page she desired.

The instant she found the page, Oona could feel the extra magic disconnect, as if the house had done its duty and now retreated of its own accord.

"Extraordinary," she said, marveling at the house's intelligence even more than its powers.

"Rather," Deacon said excitedly as he landed upon the book and began scanning the open pages. "This is exactly what we were looking for. You found it."

"The house found it," Oona corrected, and then thought: *Now, let's just hope it's helpful.*

One hour later, Oona stood in the front garden along with her uncle and Samuligan. Deacon stood resolutely upon the ironwork fence that surrounded the extensive grounds. He seemed more confident today than he had before the previous tests, and Oona guessed that it was because of what they had read in the book. Deacon put a lot of stock in what was found in books. Perhaps too much.

Oona wasn't so confident. The book had not given her any information to feel confident about.

She recalled Deacon reading the book entry aloud in the library: "The third battle test given to the Wizard's apprentice shall take him or her deeper into the world of magic than they have ever traveled before. The apprentice will enter into it wholly and from there must find their way back."

Oona had nodded. "Yes, go on."

Deacon shook his head. "I'm afraid there is nothing more to read."

Oona's mouth had flattened into an incredulous line. "Well, that isn't very helpful."

Deacon had seemed to think that it was quite helpful, explaining that it at least told her what to expect. But Oona had plopped down in a chair feeling quite disappointed. Deacon may have found it helpful, but he was not the one who was going to be tested. The entry had been exceedingly vague, and now, an hour later, she felt more anxious than ever.

Peering around at the chaos of the front garden, Oona began to wonder what the book had meant by: "The apprentice will enter into it wholly and from there must find their way back."

The overgrown plants loomed all around her, shading her partially from the sun. At her feet, thick strings of thorny vines and blankets of dry leaves covered the dark earth. The front yard was not a place she regularly visited, save for venturing to and from the front gates.

Unlike the inner garden, which existed within the walled courtyard inside Pendulum House, magical plants did not inhabit the front garden. Here the plant life was of a nonenchanted variety, and yet, to Oona, the overgrown oak trees and thorn-filled blackberry bushes had always seemed more ominous than any of the enchanted plants in the inner courtyard. And though the Wizard sometimes trimmed his rosebushes, the rest of the garden had not been tended in a very long time.

Her uncle shook his sleeves back from his wrists. "Today we will test your ability to tell illusion from reality. It is a skill that will come in handy if you should ever find yourself facing the likes of a faerie warrior."

He gestured toward Samuligan, who gave a tip of his hat.

"Sometimes," the Wizard said, "an illusion can seem more real than reality itself."

Oona frowned at this. She did not like the idea of something that was not real appearing to be more real than something that was.

To her further confusion, Samuligan grinned at her and added: "And, of course, in the end, the illusion is a part of reality; otherwise, you would not be able to experience it."

The Wizard shook his head. "Now, now, Samuligan, you're only going to confuse her."

Samuligan stood up straight and clicked the heels of his boots together. "I thought that was my job."

"I...oh, yes...so it is," the Wizard said, and shrugged apologetically at Oona. "Whatever you do, just don't panic."

"Panic?" Oona said, already feeling a bit panicky. "Why would I panic?"

Uncle Alexander placed a reassuring hand on her shoulder. "Just keep your head. Your job is to find your way back here, to me, in the garden. Back to where you are now. Remember that. Link with the house's magic. It will guide you, but you must trust the magic...not Samuligan's illusion. Remember, just find your way back to me, in the garden."

Oona shook her head, quite confused. "But why? Where am I going?"

Samuligan all at once raised his hands above his head and said: "To Faerie!"

He snapped his fingers, and suddenly the garden was gone, and so was the house, and so were the Wizard and Deacon. Only she and Samuligan remained.

The two of them stood facing each other in some kind of large stone entrance hall, like the entrance to a castle. To her left, an enormous set of double doors rose to meet the high ceiling. Two sets of thick beams set in metal brackets barred the doors shut.

To her right, a short stone stair case led up to another set of doors, these much smaller than the ones to her left. Though the doors at the top of the stairs were closed, Oona did not get the impression that they were locked. She did not know how she knew this, but she did.

As if to prove her correct, the doors to the right swung open and the sound of murmuring voices spilled through. A tall man in a black evening jacket stepped across the threshold. He held a tall metal staff in his right hand, and when he banged it against the floor, the sound was like an enormous church bell had been rung.

It was then that Oona noticed the figure's pointed ears, which were like Samuligan's. This was no man, but a faerie. Oona's mouth fell open as she looked from the faerie with the staff to Samuligan and back again. It was astonishing. Samuligan the Fay was the only faerie Oona had ever seen. Indeed, he was supposedly the only living faerie this side of the Glass Gates...unless...

Oona's brow furrowed. Was it possible—truly possible—that Samuligan had actually transported them to the Land of Faerie?

No, it's an illusion, Oona told herself, and yet, despite the thought, she did not believe it. What she believed was what she saw.

"The queen will see you," the faerie with the staff announced.

"The queen?" Oona asked.

Much as Samuligan had done in the garden, the faerie

clicked his heels together and said: "All hail the all mighty Queen Mimm the Second, Absolute Ruler of Faerie. You may enter."

Oona's mouth went dry. She tried to swallow, but found it momentarily impossible.

It's an illusion, she told herself, but once again she did not believe it.

"After you," Samuligan said, and for once he was not wearing his sly smile; instead, he showed an expression of utmost seriousness. It made Oona feel even more nervous than she already did.

Samuligan extended his hand toward the open door, and the two of them began to make their way up the stairs to be received by the queen.

The room was like no other Oona had ever been in. The ceiling soared high above and seemed to be made entirely of light. Enormous stone pillars supported the roof, and yet the stone seemed to glow, casting iridescent light upon the walls, walls that moved like water. Oona could see thousands of sparkling beings swimming within the walls, like tiny underwater pixies.

As Oona and Samuligan made their entrance, she became aware of other faeries in the room...and yet all Oona could see of them were their hands and their heads. It was both peculiar and startling to behold.

Catching sight of Oona's startled expression, Samuligan leaned down and whispered: "Invisible clothing. It was the height of fashion some five hundred years ago in the Faerie Royal Court. Many of these courtiers have very little to do. They are a lazy bunch of faeries, and they have grown quite fat. So they wear clothes that make their bodies invisible to hide their excessive weight."

Oona ran a nervous hand through her hair, looking around at the floating heads and hands. "That's the silliest thing I've ever heard."

Samuligan raised a finger to his lips. "Don't let them hear you say that. They believe that invisibility is the paramount of fashion."

Speaking of fashion, Oona noticed that many of the male faeries wore cowboy hats similar to the one Samuligan wore. Even more curious was the fact that no one seemed to have noticed Oona and Samuligan's arrival. Despite the fact that the two of them were the most visible people there, it was as if Samuligan and Oona were the ones no one could see.

"Wait a minute," Oona said as the two of them walked down the center of the long throne room. "This is the past, isn't it, Samuligan? This is how you remember Faerie."

Samuligan did not answer but instead picked up his pace. Oona hurried to keep up with the faerie's long strides. The room seemed to go on for miles, and yet their pace was much faster than Oona could normally have managed. It was as if some force were speeding them along. The floating heads and hands of the courtiers began to blur past.

They walked for what might have been ten minutes before Oona saw any indication of an end. Her breath suddenly caught in her throat as the throne came into view, though calling it simply a throne did not do it justice. It was in actuality a tree...a massive tree whose limbs and branches glowed with the same intensity as the ceiling above.

And then it occurred to Oona that the ceiling actually *was* the branches and limbs of the tree, which weaved a giant canopy of beams high overhead. The result was breathtaking, giving the effect that the throne, or more aptly the person sitting on the throne, was the source of all of that immense light.

Quite suddenly, Oona found herself standing before the Queen of the Fay in all of her terrible beauty. Unlike her courtiers, the queen's attire was clearly visible and startlingly simple. Her long black dress appeared blacker than was possible, and Oona took a step back at the sight of it for fear that she might tumble into it and be lost forever within its darkness.

From her high throne, the queen stared down upon them with eyes as bright as stars, her expression one of imperious indifference. And though Oona would have easily admitted that the queen was the most beautiful being she had ever laid eyes upon—her facial features appeared perfect, her posture relaxed and regal, her dark skin unblemished in any way—Oona also couldn't help but feel that there was something quite disturbing about her. It was as if she were too perfect.

"As if she were not real..." Oona said beneath her breath.

Samuligan knelt before the throne. "Your Majesty," he said, and even in just those two words Oona could hear the reverence he held for this awe-inspiring figure.

"Samuligan," the queen replied, her voice smooth and full of power. "My most loyal general. I see you have brought the girl."

"I have," he said.

"She looks so...small."

Oona opened her mouth to protest, but the queen held up one hand, and Oona found she could not speak.

"Is she ready?" the queen asked

"We shall see," Samuligan said.

The queen nodded her agreement and turned her gaze upon Oona. Her eyes were like two monstrous beasts, dark and terrible to behold. Oona could not have said why, but holding the queen's gaze was the hardest thing she had ever done. Strange that it should be so...and yet there was no denying the truth of it. It seemed to Oona that the queen could see all the way into the bottom of her, to where her greatest fears slept in the shadowy corners of her mind. She felt them all stir at once, and panic seized hold of her chest.

She wanted more than anything to look away from those dark, cruel eyes, to close her own eyes from the terror that lived there, but she could not look away. She was trapped like a fly in the faerie queen's web. She tried to scream, but no sound came from her lips.

Just when Oona felt she could not take one single second more, the queen turned her gaze away, almost as if she were bored. Oona felt her breath fill her chest in a great gasp, and her knees shook unsteadily beneath her own weight.

"She is full of fear, this one. I think she needs to grow." The queen clapped her hands twice, the sound like dueling thunderclaps. Without warning, the tree throne upon which the queen sat came alive. Its enormous limbs began to descend from the ceiling like hundreds of fingers reaching out for Oona.

Oona screamed and turned to run. She had to get out of here. But the instant she spun around, she found that the invisible courtiers blocked her way. She tried to push past them—pushing against what looked like nothing at all, but felt like large, heavily clad bodies—and found it impossible. They muttered incoherently, shaking their heads as if she should know better.

Her heart began to pound heavily in her chest as she whirled around, looking for some other place of escape. Her eyes caught on a door to her left. The door was closed, but she rushed to it nonetheless, certain that at any moment she would feel the grip of those wriggling tentacle-like tree branches clap hold of her arms.

She threw herself at the door and hammered down the latch. To her surprise, it opened, and she shoved blindly through, slamming the door shut behind her. Her breath heaved in her chest as she took in her new surroundings. To her horror, she found that she had pushed her way through the doorway only to find herself standing in the very same room she had just left.

"Oh, dear," she said. "This is not good at all."

Samuligan stood to her right, near the queen, while the partially invisible courtiers closed in from her left. The tree limbs continued their horrifying descent from the high ceiling, now mere feet from her.

"It's like a bad dream," she said to no one in particular...and then a thought occurred to her.

It is exactly *like a dream.* And dreams, of course, were nothing but...

"Illusion," she said.

"Don't be so sure," Samuligan said with a casual tip of his hat.

But this time Oona was sure. It had to be an illusion...all of it. The Glass Gates had been closed for more than five hundred years, barring the way to Faerie. Not even Samuligan could travel between the worlds...despite the fact that it all seemed so real.

"Whatever you do, don't panic," her uncle had said, which was exactly what she had done. She had panicked and pushed through the door, and it had gotten her exactly nowhere. Oona couldn't help but wonder if there was a lesson to be learned in that.

She felt a moment of defiance, and it occurred to her that she might just stand there and let the descending tree branches take her. If they were an illusion, surely they could not hurt her. But that thought passed just as quickly as it had come. Her mind believed that what was happening was real, and doing nothing was not an option.

I need to link with the house, she thought. *But I'm in Faerie...how can I link with Pendulum House?* She shook her head, trying to clear it. *I'm not in Faerie. I'm in the Pendulum House front garden. This is all an illusion.*

The first of the descending branches caught hold of her and jerked her arm up. The pain in her shoulder was sharp, and she wondered briefly how it was possible that an illusion could cause her pain.

I can feel it, she thought. Not only could she feel the bite of pain in her shoulder, she could feel the slithering fingers of the oncoming branches as they wrapped around her legs and arms, lifting her into the air. She let out a yelp of surprise and fear. The strength within the glowing branches was tremendous; they were going to tear her apart, she just knew it.

"Find your way back to me in the garden," her uncle had said. "Back to where you are, now."

"I am in the garden," she told herself, though she did not believe it. "In the Pendulum House front garden. *Profundus magicus!*"

The effect was instantaneous. Distracted as she was with the illusionary world that surrounded her, Oona's mind filled with the knowledge she needed to overcome it. It was an ancient knowledge far more powerful than the thin deception Samuligan was playing on her. And to her surprise, it was not so much a spell but a song. A wordless song, but one of tremendous beauty.

She opened her mouth and sang a single syllable, first rising and then falling in a gorgeous melody that seemed to come from out of her very bones. The sound penetrated every part of her being, resonating and harmonizing with everything it touched. Never before had Oona sung so unabashedly, so openly, and so passionately.

For a brief moment, Adler Iree's face swam before her eyes, and her mother's face, and that of her baby sister Flora...and her father. Suddenly, the light that emanated from the tree limbs began to crack. Her song rose in energy and her pitch shifted even higher, now a haunting banshee cry, and the limbs shattered like glass. The queen and her throne room full of courtiers vaporized into nothingness, and now it was the Wizard's face that she saw before her.

This was no illusion. The white puffy clouds dotted the purplish-blue sky behind where he stood in the front garden, surrounded by the thorny rosebushes. Samuligan stood nearby, just as he had before they had entered the Faerie Royal Court.

She had done it. She had managed to find her way back.

The house led me back, she thought, and then all at once she realized that she was still singing. Her mouth closed abruptly, and her face flushed. Hands feeling quite shaky, she let out a heavy sigh, her heart rate only just beginning to slow.

"Extraordinary," Samuligan said. He peered at her, eyebrows raised in an expression of surprise—a rarity for the faerie.

"Back so soon?" the Wizard said, looking equally impressed.

"Soon?" Oona said. Her voice trembled slightly from the effects of the magic. "I thought we were gone for quite some time. I mean...it was all so real. We were there, weren't we, Samuligan? We traveled to Faerie."

"We did, indeed," Samuligan said, and tapped the side of his head. "We traveled through our thoughts."

"Illusion," the Wizard said. "Nothing more."

Oona shook her head, not so sure. She could still remember the grip of the tree limbs around her wrists and arms. She recalled the cold stare of the faerie queen and shivered. It had been real...she had been there...and yet the house's magic had shattered that reality like a broken window, exposing the true reality behind it.

"Is this one real?" Oona asked, looking around the garden, eyes wide with confusion. She could see Deacon perched just as he had been, upon the ironwork fence that surrounded the grounds. He extended his wings and flew to her shoulder. She felt the familiar grip of his talons on her shoulder...and yet the grip of the tree had seemed just as true.

"It is an excellent question," the Wizard said. "Once one illusion has been broken, it is only natural to question the validity of everything else we see, smell, hear, taste, and touch. All of our senses are susceptible to illusion, which is why learning to discern what is real and what is not is an essential skill needed by any Wizard. You have done remarkably well. I, myself, was lost in an alternate reality for nearly twenty-four hours before I was able to connect with the house's magic and break free. It seemed more like a month to me. You, Oona, were lost for less than a minute."

"A minute?" Oona asked, surprised to hear it. "Surely, I was there at least...twenty minutes."

Samuligan stretched his long faerie arms and looked as if he were about to yawn. "Time is an illusion...no matter how you look at it."

Oona frowned at this. She did not like the idea of existing in any kind of illusion, faerie fabricated or not. It was logic, and reason, and facts that she relied upon to hold her world together like glue...but in a world filled with magic, she knew that that glue did not always hold.

Chapter Eleven

The Mortenstine Building

Knots: The Art of Abraham McGillicuddy was fascinating. Filled with beautifully illustrated versions of every knot, it was no wonder the book was kept in the art section of the library.

Oona propped herself up in bed and flipped through its pages in the low light from the magical glow globe. She wondered who, besides the creator of the book, would have known how to tie the Rose Knot.

"Now there's a thought," she said, and turned to the back page, expecting to find a biography of the author. To her disappointment, however, there was nothing of the sort to be found.

"What does the *Who's Who* have to say about Abraham McGillicuddy, Deacon?" Oona asked.

Deacon, who was presently settling down for the night atop Oona's dressing table mirror, jumped at the mention of his name. "Hmm? What? Aren't we asleep yet?" He blinked several times as if coming awake.

Oona stared at him expectantly. "Abraham McGillicuddy, Deacon. In the *Who's Who*."

"Oh, yes...of course." He paused a moment, checking

through his mental files, before replying: "Hmm."

"Hmm?" Oona questioned.

"Hmm," Deacon sounded again, before adding: "There is no record of an Abraham McGillicuddy ever having lived on Dark Street. He must have lived in the World of Mmm—" He stopped abruptly and cleared his throat. "That is to say, the World of Humans."

Oona nodded approvingly at his use of the word *humans*, but then frowned when she realized what he was saying. "You mean to tell me that the man who wrote this book didn't even live on Dark Street?"

Deacon nodded, though not very enthusiastically. His eyelids appeared to droop and his beak dropped toward his wing as he stifled a yawn. "It's possible he could have visited, but there is no magical record of his having lived here."

Oona flipped to the front of the book and found the fine print at the bottom of the title page: *Published by Gordson & Gool—1838.*

"What about Gordson and Gool, the publishers?" she asked. "Are they from Dark Street?"

Again, Deacon paused. "There was a Maxwell Gordson who lived on Dark Street, but he died over a hundred years ago, and he was a leather tanner, not a publisher. My guess is that they were New York publishers. Perhaps we should come back to this in the morning. Aren't you tired from your test?"

Oona slapped the book shut and sighed. The truth was she felt exhausted, yet her mind would not let her rest. It kept looping again and again over the same incomprehensible thought ever since she had returned from Faerie. And that was exactly the problem...she had not actually gone to Faerie, and yet her mind insisted that she had. It had been an illusion that seemed more real than her everyday life.

This created a kind of paradox in her brain that insisted everything around her was both real and not real at the same time. Upon entering her room that evening, she had picked up and put down her hairbrush several times, contemplating if she were really holding it or not. She had done the same thing earlier in the evening with her soupspoon at the dinner table. Her uncle had assured her that such feelings were to be expected, and that they would soon pass, but presently she found the only cure was to concentrate on her goal of finding her father's killers.

"The night watchman," she said.

"I beg pardon?" Deacon asked.

"The night watchman at the museum. The man who was tied up."

"Elbert Hackelsmith?" Deacon asked.

Oona ran a hand through her hair, thinking aloud. "We should pay him a visit—ask him if it is at all possible that he *misheard* the thief."

Deacon adjusted his position upon the mirror, his talons clicking against the wood frame. "You are referring to your theory that the male voice that the night watchman heard saying, '*Shush*, he'll hear you,' was, in fact, saying, '*Mrs. Shusher*, he'll hear you."

Oona nodded thoughtfully. "Hackelsmith did say that his ears were still ringing from the blow to his head. Does the *Who's Who* give his address?"

Deacon yawned. "I hope you aren't planning on visiting him tonight."

"Don't be silly, Deacon. First thing in the morning should suffice."

Deacon shrugged and spoke in a far-off voice, as if he were already drifting into dreamland. "Well, I don't know his address. With the exception of very famous people, the *Who's Who* does not keep track of residences."

Oona slumped in her bed, wondering how she might go about finding Mr. Hackelsmith's home.

The following morning Oona found herself once again trudging up the museum steps. Deacon stretched his wings upon her shoulder and squinted against the morning light. The sun was just cresting the tops of the buildings and lighting up their brick facades like fire.

That feeling of unreality that she had suffered the previous night had mostly disappeared—*mostly*, but not completely. A few times during the carriage ride to the museum she had questioned whether or not the smell of baking bread or the sound of horse hooves clopping on the cobblestones were real sensations or just illusions. But the feelings had passed more quickly than they had the previous night, and for that Oona was thankful.

The museum steps felt quite solid and real beneath her feet.

"Will you tell me now why we must be here so early?" Deacon asked. "It's just now seven o'clock. The museum doesn't open until nine o'clock."

Oona pointed to the uniformed man ascending the steps just in front of them. It was Victor the day guard arriving for work.

"Because, Deacon," Oona said, "this is the time the night shift changes over to the day shift. We can catch Mr. Hackelsmith, the night watchman, on his way home, and ask about what he heard the night of the theft."

But to Oona's dismay, it was not Hackelsmith who opened the front door and stepped over the threshold to greet Victor, but it was someone completely new. The two men— Victor the day guard and the uniformed stranger—greeted each other as the stranger placed a set of keys into Victor's open hand.

"Where is Elbert Hackelsmith?" Oona demanded.

Both men turned in surprise. They stared at her for a

long moment, and then Victor the day guard shook his head. "Oh, it's you again. Sorry, but Elbert's staying at home this week. Doctor's orders. This here is Dezmond, our alternate night watchman."

"What's this all about?" Dezmond asked. A thin, gray-haired man with tufts of white hair coming out of his nose, the night watchman peered down the sides of his nose at her with irritation.

"Oh, this is Miss Crate," Victor said appealingly. "Fancies herself to be a bit of a detective, don't ya?"

Oona ignored the question. "Do you know where he lives?"

"Dezmond?" Victor asked, surprised.

Oona shook her head. "No, not Dezmond. Elbert Hackelsmith."

"Matter of fact, I do," Victor said. "Mr. Glump asked me to take Elbert's paycheck to him when I left yesterday. He lives in the Mortenstine Building, third floor. Number eighteen, I think."

"Hey, why are you giving out private information?" Dezmond asked disapprovingly.

"Who said it was private?" Victor replied.

"I just hope you don't go giving out *my* personal information," Dezmond snapped.

"I don't even know where you live. And besides, who are you to tell me what..."

The sound of the two men arguing faded as Oona made her way quickly back to the curb, where Samuligan waited patiently atop the carriage. She climbed inside and called out: "Take us to the Mortenstine Building, Samuligan."

Twenty minutes later they came to a halt in front of a dingy-looking four-story building. As Oona stepped to the curb she peered across the street at the golden facade of the Nightshade Hotel and Casino. It was there, within the hotel's expensive walls, that Red Martin had run his criminal

148

organization for years, without anyone other than his most devout followers ever getting so much as a glimpse of the man.

"Do you think he is inside?" Oona asked.

"You mean Red Martin?" Deacon asked. "I should think not. He is wanted by the police now."

"True," Oona said, yet she could not shake the feeling that someone was watching her. She shifted her attention and stared up at the ominously face of the Mortenstine Building. A sudden chill rolled over her. Festooned with crumbly gargoyles and grimy ledges, the building reminded Oona that she had read of more than one crime happening within its darkened walls.

"Shall I accompany you?" Samuligan asked, and when Oona turned, she discovered that he was already standing beside her.

"That sounds like a good idea to me," Deacon said, and Oona could feel his talons clamp down harder than was necessary upon her shoulder. As if unable to contain the encyclopedic knowledge in his head, he added: "The Mortenstine Building is named after Mortimer Mortenstine, a well-known magician from the 1600s. The very Mortenstine who wrote *Mortenstine's Monstrous Conspectus*. He was obsessed with monsters and creatures of the dark. Though he was never given the title Wizard of Dark Street—at the time that honor belonged to Antwerp Orbiter—it is said that Mortenstine had even greater influence on Dark Street than the Wizard himself did. He was also quite a controversial figure for openly dabbling in dark magic."

Samuligan made a *tsk* sound. "Mortimer Mortenstine did more than dabble."

Oona looked up at the faerie, curious. "How do you mean?"

Samuligan shrugged. "I have lived on Dark Street for nearly five hundred years and have seen my share of magicians who experimented with the darker side of magic.

But none who I can think of ever went so far down into that darkness than Mortimer Mortenstine. In the end, it destroyed him."

"What happened?" Oona asked, though she was not sure she really wanted to know. Her uncle had shared several terrible stories of those who worked with dark magic, none of them ending well.

Deacon cleared his throat. "Mortenstine had many enemies, one of whom was Antwerp Orbiter, the Wizard. As you know, it is the presiding Wizard's job to handle magical wrongdoing, and it is believed that Mortenstine was trying to summon some kind of horrendous monster to kill the Wizard. At that point, Mortenstine was apparently so steeped in the dark arts that he had gone completely mad. But the summoning spell he attempted was too much for him to handle."

Deacon fell silent.

Oona peered sidelong at him. "Go on."

Samuligan clapped his hands together and a puff of smoke plumed above his touching thumbs. The smoke formed what looked like a mouth full of razor-sharp teeth. "He was eaten by the very creature he summoned."

Oona took in a startled breath. "He was...eaten?" She paused briefly to consider the horror of it, and then shook her head. "Why would anyone name a building after such a lunatic?"

"No one did," Samuligan said. "This building just happens to be built on the very spot where Mortenstine's house once stood; the very place where he conducted so many of his dark spells, and where he attempted to summon his monster. When this residential building was first constructed one hundred years ago, it was originally named the Palace Flats. The name was carved in stone above the entrance, but the day after the stone was put into place, the name had mysteriously changed to the Mortenstine Building. The stone was removed and redone, once again with the name the Palace Flats, but the following day the name had once more become the Mortenstine Building."

Oona peered up at the grimy stone above the door and read the name engraved there. A shiver snaked along her arms as she thought of the dark magic that had carved it. And then an even more disturbing thought occurred to her.

"What about the monster?" she asked. "The one that ate Mortenstine. What became of it?"

Samuligan shrugged, and then peered up at the building. Oona followed his gaze. The gargoyles along the ledges seemed to be staring down upon them with malicious eyes.

"No one knows," Deacon replied. "Perhaps it returned to whence it came...after it feasted."

Oona grimaced. "Perhaps?"

"Perhaps," Samuligan replied matter-of-factly. He moved toward the front entrance to the building. "Shall we?"

Oona took in a steadying breath and followed.

Deacon said: "I believe you should be more concerned about running into unsavory characters than Mortenstine's monster. This building is notorious for housing shady criminals."

"We'll be safe with Samuligan," Oona said, though her throat had gone quite dry.

They pushed through the front door and entered a dark entryway. Though two large windows exposed the entryway to daylight, the room seemed unnaturally dark. The dirty green walls were peeling away in places, and so far as Oona could tell, none of the wall sconces were in working order. The smells of mold and dust filled the air, along with the stench of rotting trash, and as she peered down the long hallway before them, she saw several rodents scurry across the filthy carpet and disappear into a hole.

Oona shook her head in disgust. "Why would anyone with a decent-paying job live in such a place?"

"You can ask Mr. Hackelsmith yourself," Samuligan

said, and moved to the left. A darkened stairwell spiraled to the upper floors. The three of them ascended the rickety wooden steps, rusty nails creaking with each step.

Oona's heart gave a heavy thump when she stepped upon the second-story landing and saw what appeared to be an enormous snake coiled upon the floor. She stepped back in surprise, nearly slipping down the stairs before realizing that what she was looking at was not a giant snake but a human body lying in the corner. The body was dressed in clothes made entirely of snakeskin.

Seeing the body was startling enough, but when the body moved, Oona leapt onto Samuligan's back for safety. Deacon shot from her shoulder and landed on the faerie's cowboy hat.

"Hello chap," the man on the floor said. "Want to buy a magic fring...I mean ring...I mean...yeah, ringy?"

He held up his hand, wiggling his ringless fingers.

"I see no ring," Samuligan said.

"It's invisible, so it is. Enchanted!" the man replied.

"What does it do?" Samuligan asked, now sounding quite amused. Oona wished he would just move quickly on.

"What does it do?" the man on the floor asked indignantly. "I'll tell you what it does. It gives you whatever you fish for...hiccup...I mean *wish* for!"

"Ridiculous," Deacon said. "Never has such a ring existed."

Samuligan cocked his head to one side, looking down at the man in the snakeskin suit, and spoke quite earnestly. "And what, pray tell, did *you* wish for, good sir?"

The man sat up slightly, propping himself against the wall with his left hand and holding himself steady with a green glass bottle in his right. Oona could see his eyes look about as he tried to think of a quick answer. He took a thoughtful swig from the green bottle and nodded.

"I wished for this fine alligator suit," the man said, and then smiled as if he were quite clever.

"The suit you are wearing is clearly made of snakeskin," Deacon said pompously. "Not alligator skin."

The man looked down at his suit, feigning surprise. "Oswald's fury! Look at that, so it is. This ring must be faulty. But still, I'll sell it to you half frice...I mean...hiccup...half price. Now that's a deal."

"We will pass," Oona said sternly as she released her grip from Samuligan and dropped to the floor. "Shall we go, Samuligan?"

The faerie nodded, but instead of continuing up the stairs, he knelt down beside the man on the floor.

"I'll make *you* a deal," Samuligan said. "I'll give you my ring for yours."

The faerie reached into his pocket and brought out what appeared to be a solid gold ring. It gleamed brightly, despite the lack of light in the stairwell. There was something not right about the ring, Oona noticed, but she couldn't quite tell what it was.

The man in the snakeskin suit's eyes went wide and he sat up perfectly straight. "You got a deal!"

The man pretended to remove the invisible ring from his hand. He held it up and held out his open palm. "On the count of three we exchange."

Samuligan nodded and held out his own hand. "One, two...three."

As the golden ring fell from Samuligan's pinched fingers into the man's hand, it seemed to lose its solidity. Indeed, by the time it reached the man's open palm, it had vanished completely. Contrarily, the fake ring that the man pretended to drop onto Samuligan's palm did quite the opposite, gaining solidity as it fell, so that by the time it touched the faerie's skin, the ring was a solid piece of silver.

"Hey, what gives?" the man protested. He made as if to stand, but then just as quickly slid back down the wall. "You tricked me!"

Samuligan smiled broadly. "Not at all. I gave you a

gold illusion for a silver one. I'd say the one you have now is worth quite a bit more than the one I have now."

The man frowned, clenching his fingers around the emptiness in his hand. He suddenly sounded more sober than he had only a minute before. "But one illusion isn't worth more than another. They're both just illusions."

"Are they?" Samuligan asked philosophically. He turned to Oona, eyebrows raised.

The look sparked something in her, a realization that she had known from the instant he had pulled out the golden ring. She had *known* it was an illusion before it had even disappeared. Her eyes had still been fooled...but she had known something was off. It had not been real. Unlike the day before, when she had traveled through Samuligan's faerie illusion and gotten completely lost in the belief of its fantastic reality, this time she had sensed the flaw.

Samuligan seemed to read the realization on her face. "You learn fast, Miss Crate. You will be a great Wizard."

He turned and began moving up the steps to the third floor. Deacon returned to Oona's shoulder, and the two of them quickly followed the faerie, leaving the man in the snakeskin suit behind with a baffled expression on his heavily lined face.

"Who's there?" a voice asked from behind the door.

Oona had knocked several times upon the door of number eighteen, and was just about to give up when the voice sounded from the other side.

"Is that you, Mr. Hackelsmith?" Oona asked. "It is I, Oona Crate."

The sound of several locks could be heard unbolting, followed by the creak of rusty hinges as the door swung inward. Elbert Hackelsmith stood in the doorway in a set of well-worn sleeping pajamas. He looked bleary-eyed, and his hair stuck out in different directions as if he had just awoken.

"Oh, hello," he said, his expression one of mild surprise at finding a thirteen-year-old girl with a raven on her shoulder standing in his hallway. He looked around suspiciously and discovered Samuligan standing nearby looking rather ominous in his long black cloak. The faerie gave a nod of the head and Hackelsmith shuddered. He then peered past Samuligan down the hall before bringing his gaze back to Oona.

"I thought you might have been the landlord when you first knocked," he said. "Don't like it when he comes around. Creepy sort of bloke. Always in the same snakeskin suit."

Oona blinked several times in surprise. "You mean that man in the stairwell is the landlord of this building?"

Hackelsmith scratched nervously at the back of his head. "Sounds like him. He try to sell you a magic ring?"

"As a matter of fact, he did," Oona replied.

Hackelsmith nodded. "That's him. Don't like him much, myself...but I try to stay on his best side. He is the landlord, after all. Anyway, you're welcome to come in if you like."

He stepped aside and Oona could see past him into the room beyond. The room was quite dark, with no direct sunlight entering through the windows because Hackelsmith had hung several layers of ragged towels over the glass. As her eyes wandered over the scene, Oona spotted what could only have been the corner of a coffin sticking out from around the edge of the short entryway.

Oona swallowed a lump in her throat and thought: *If he thinks I'm going in there, he's mad.*

And now that she looked at him, Mr. Hackelsmith did look a bit...not crazy, that was not the word...but she was fairly certain she had seen that look before. But where?

You've seen it before in the eyes of stray dogs, a voice in her head said. *That's where you've seen it.*

And then she realized what the look was. It was hunger. It was strange, but Oona had a sudden idea of what a potpie might feel like. She squinted at Hackelsmith's dim face, and he smiled faintly at her...and that is when she saw the teeth. Not exactly fangs...or were they? It was hard to tell, but they definitely seemed pointy—pointier than a normal person's teeth would have been—and all at once the bone-chilling thought that Mortenstine's monster had never been found barged into Oona's mind like an uninvited guest.

That's ridiculous, Oona thought. *That was hundreds of years ago.*

Still, Oona made no move to enter the apartment, even with Samuligan's accompaniment.

"I have only come to ask one quick question," Oona said, and was surprised to hear a slight quaver in her own voice.

Was that disappointment she saw on the night watchman's face? She could not tell.

"Yeah, all right, what's this all about?" he asked, and stepped forward into the hall, crossing his long muscular arms but keeping his slight smile.

Now that he had come into the light of the hallway, Oona realized that his teeth were not truly pointy at all.

Did I imagine it? she wondered, but on second consideration she believed that she had not. His teeth, she was most certain, had changed.

Wishing simply to turn and make a run for it, Oona forced herself to stand her ground, reminding herself that Samuligan was there, and that he would not let anything happen to her.

"Is it possible that you misheard what the male thief said to the female thief at the museum?" She spoke so quickly that it took Hackelsmith a moment to comprehend what she had said.

"Misheard? What do you mean?" he asked.

"I mean, is it possible that the male thief might have

actually said, '*Mrs. Shusher*, he'll hear you,' instead of, '*Shush*, he'll hear you'?"

Hackelsmith's face pinched up, as if he had just bitten into a sour lemon. "Mrs. Shusher? You mean the librarian? I don't think so. I mean...anything's possible, my ears were ringing from getting knocked on the back of the head, it's true...but I heard the voice quite clearly. Why are you asking about all of this, anyway? You're too young to be working for the police."

But Oona was already turning to go. She had an overwhelming urge to get as far away from the Mortenstine Building as she could manage. "Thank you, Mr. Hackelsmith. That's all I needed to know. Sorry to disturb you."

"Hey!" Hackelsmith said, and he reached out a hand as if to stop Oona from leaving, but a sound like that of thunder cracked in the hall, echoing off the walls and shaking the floor. Hackelsmith cried out in pain.

Oona glanced back to see what had happened, only to discover Hackelsmith cradling his closed fist. Thin tendrils of what looked like steam rose from the back of his hand.

"That hurt, it did!" Hackelsmith said, looking accusingly at the faerie servant.

Samuligan placed his hand on Oona's shoulder and turned her in the direction of the stairs. "Let us depart, Miss Crate."

"Yes, let's," Oona said as various doors along the hallway opened and heads poked out to see what was causing all of the noise.

"I'll tell the police about this!" Hackelsmith called after them, but to Oona it sounded like an empty threat. She had a feeling he would not want the police to come snooping around his creepy apartment.

They descended the stairwell, stepping over the slumped landlord, and less than a minute later emerged from the building onto the front sidewalk. Oona stopped beside the carriage and peered up toward the third floor, to where she thought Hackelsmith's apartment was located.

"You know, I believe that night watchman might be a vampire," she said.

"Vampire?" Deacon said. He paused a moment to check his memory. "There's no mention of it in the *Dark Street Who's Who*. But then again, many vampires go their entire lives without their secret being discovered. They excrete a kind of chemical when they bite their victims that make them forget who it was who bit them. The victims often wake up in strange places, wondering what happened. It is, of course, extremely rare that vampires will actually kill their victims, choosing instead to feed off the same prey for as long as they can...like returning to a favorite restaurant."

Oona squinched up her face in disgust. And then a thought occurred to her: "Do you think that's what happened to the landlord? Mr. Hackelsmith did say he did not like him."

Samuligan looked skeptical as he climbed to the top of the carriage, but then shrugged. He did not seem much interested.

"Well, I'll be sure to let Inspector White know my suspicions all the same," Oona said, before adding: "Not that it will do any good." She frowned. "And the whole thing was just a waste of time anyway. Hackelsmith's answer was no help at all."

"You mean that it was not what you wanted to hear," Deacon said pompously from her shoulder.

Oona decided to ignore this and instead turned her attention to the newspaper stand up the street. The stand seemed quite busy, with pedestrians of all sorts jostling to get their hands on a copy of the paper. Having risen so early this morning, she had not had a chance to peruse the *Dark Street Tribune* to see if anything had been printed about Molly Morgana Moon's political rally and the ensuing riot.

She approached the stand, sliding between two men in expensive business suits, only to discover that the entire front page of the newspaper was devoted to the riot. She snatched up a copy and scanned the cover image. An illustration of Molly Morgana Moon's smiling face stared out from the top page, just below the headline: OVERNIGHT POLLS PUT MOLLY MORGANA MOON IN LEAD.

Oona shook her head, confused. "But voting day isn't until tomorrow. How can she be in the lead when voting hasn't even begun yet?"

"Because," Deacon said, "it is just a poll taken by the newspaper. They ask a small portion of the population who they are going to vote for by sending reporters door to door to ask. It is not definitive."

"But this is wonderful news," Oona said. Her eyes were already scanning the first few paragraphs in the article. "It seems that Tobias Fink's plan to disrupt yesterday's rally backfired when word about the riot spread throughout the street. And now look, it's even on the front of the *Dark Street Tribune*."

Deacon, who was a much faster reader than Oona, scanned the article as well. After a moment he said: "But Tobias Fink denies having anything to do with the riot or the protesters."

"Of course he does, Deacon," Oona said. "But he's obviously lying. We saw those men carrying signs that said 'Fink for Council.'"

Deacon continued to read. "Fink is accusing Molly Morgana Moon of paying the thugs herself. He says that the whole thing was staged."

"To what end?" Oona asked.

"To gain attention," Deacon said. "For publicity."

Oona shook her head disbelievingly.

"Hey, you!" said the bearded man behind the newspaper stand. "You gonna pay for that or what?"

"Oh, sorry," Oona said, and put the paper back where she had found it. "There'll be a copy at home, I'm sure."

"Then off with you," the bearded man said with a shooing gesture.

Oona slipped through the crowd and headed back toward the Mortenstine Building, only to find yet another crowd forming around Samuligan and the carriage. The pedestrians had all stopped in their tracks and were watching in amazement as the faerie juggled what appeared to be three heavy granite tombstones, tossing one over the other as if they weighed no more than a set of juggling balls.

For some reason, it was the sight of the tombstones, rather than the fact that the faerie was juggling them, that caused all of the tiny hairs to stand up along her arms. To Oona, the bizarre scene was more ominous than amazing.

"What's he doing?" she asked nervously.

"Perhaps he's preparing for this afternoon's battle test," Deacon replied.

She swallowed what felt like a lump of coal in her throat. "Yes, I was afraid you would say that."

She watched the tombstones flip around and around as more spectators stopped and pointed, mesmerized by the feat. To Oona, the stones meant only one thing. The next test had to do with death...something that Oona had already had too much of in her life. She sighed heavily. "I don't like this at all."

Chapter Twelve

The Fourth Test

By midafternoon an overcast sheet of clouds had settled over the street, cooling the air considerably and obscuring the sun. Oona sat inside the Pendulum House library, looking out a window and wondering if it was going to rain.

"That's a fancy magnifying glass, so it is," said a voice.

Oona looked down at her magnifying glass, which presently lay on top of the copy of *Apprenticeship Magica*, and then looked up to find Mrs. Carlyle dusting a nearby shelf.

"Oh, yes, I suppose it is," Oona said, picking the magnifying glass up by its wooden handle and examining the golden rim. "This was my father's. It's sort of become my wand, really. It works well for me."

"Better than Oswald's wand?" Deacon asked inquisitively from his place on the table.

Oona ran her thumb over the smooth gold ring, considering the question thoughtfully. "I suppose Oswald's wand does work better as a conductor. It's more precise, if that's what you mean. But this feels more natural. More...me, if that makes any sense. Anyway, Uncle Alexander lets me use Oswald's wand only during the battle tests."

"As is only right," Deacon said. "Red Martin would still love to get his hands on it."

"Red Martin?" asked Mrs. Carlyle. "You mean the owner of the Nightshade Casino?"

"The very same," Oona said.

"Isn't he supposedly some sort of"—Mrs. Carlyle's voice dropped to a whisper, as if Red Martin himself might be standing near by, like a tiger ready to pounce—"crime lord," she finished.

"He is; no *supposedly* about it," Oona said. "He is the head of the Dark Street criminal underground. The newspaper doesn't print much about it, but I suspect that is because the editors are either afraid of him...or under his pay."

"That is simple speculation," Deacon put in before relenting: "Though it does seem likely."

Mrs. Carlyle frowned. "Can he do magic?"

She seemed quite disturbed by the idea.

Oona shook her head. "No. He can't...but he could get someone else who *can* do magic to use the wand for him."

"What, to rob people?" Mrs. Carlyle asked.

"That's one possibility," Oona said. "But what he really wants the wand for is to use it as a key. You see, Oswald used the wand to close the Glass Gates at the end of the Great Faerie War. And the wand is rumored to be the only way to open the Glass Gates again."

Mrs. Carlyle's eyes went wide. "Now why on Dark Street would he want to do that? I thought the faerie queen threatened to kill all humans. If those gates ever open..."

She trailed off.

"Red Martin thinks that if he has a key, he can more easily smuggle his illegal products across the Faerie border," Deacon said shortly. "Now, if you don't mind, Mrs.

Carlyle...Miss Crate is preparing for her most challenging test yet and needs to concentrate."

Mrs. Carlyle looked as if she were going to ask yet another question. Clearly, the maid, like most people on Dark Street, was unaware that Red Martin knew of a secret way to pass from Dark Street to the Land of Faerie. And while it was rumored that Red Martin himself was centuries old, very few people knew that this was actually true, and that he was able to accomplish this by smearing a magical plant known as turlock root on his skin, keeping him from ever growing old. The truth was, Red Martin had been smuggling his nefarious items from one world to the other for hundreds of years.

Seeing Deacon's stern posture, however, Mrs. Carlyle closed her mouth and once again resumed her dusting.

Oona was tempted to explain what she had learned from Red Martin himself...that his secret method of sneaking from one world to the other was a very slow and arduous task, and that Red Martin wished to use the wand—the only known key to the Glass Gates—to speed up his importing process.

But Oona knew that Deacon was right, and now was not the time to go into such things. She needed to concentrate. Looking down at the open book, she raised her magnifying glass to read the tiny print. "According to the *Apprenticeship Magica*, today's test is the next to last, and my ability to balance more than one task will be challenged."

"Balance more than one task, huh?" asked Mrs. Carlyle. "I prefer to do one thing at a time, I do."

"Then it's a good thing that Miss Crate is taking the test today and not you," Deacon said briskly.

"There's no need to be rude, Deacon," Oona said.

"It's all right," the maid said. "Your bird's right, even if he is a bit pretentious about it. I should leave you to it."

Unable to help herself, Oona let out a sharp laugh.

"Pretentious, am I?" Deacon said as all the feathers stood up along the back of his head.

"No, Deacon," Oona said apologetically, though there was still a hint of laughter in her voice, "we know you have the right of it. In fact, it's time to meet Samuligan and Uncle Alexander."

"Is the test happening here again, in the house?" Mrs. Carlyle asked, now sounding slightly nervous.

"I believe it is taking place outside the grounds, in the street," Deacon said.

"In the street?" said Mrs. Carlyle. "That sounds dangerous."

Oona thought of the three tombstones Samuligan had been juggling and said, rather absently: "'Deadly' is more like it."

"What?" the maid asked in alarm.

Oona shook her head and made her way toward the library doors. "Oh nothing."

"Good luck," the maid called after her.

Oona thanked her before venturing down the hall and out the front door.

She and Deacon met the Wizard and Samuligan just outside the Pendulum House front gates. The Wizard and the faerie servant sat at a round table, which had been placed in the middle of the sidewalk. The table had been set for tea.

Oona was surprised not only to find the oddity of the table on the sidewalk, but also to see Samuligan sitting in a chair. It surprised her because, though she had seen Samuligan take his seat upon the top of the carriage countless times, she had never seen him sit down in a proper chair in all of her years living at Pendulum House.

Overhead, the sky was darkening, and Oona felt quite certain rain was on its way. Because of the impending weather, the street was fairly deserted.

The Wizard gestured toward the open chair across from him. Oona took her seat as Samuligan filled her cup and pushed it in front of her.

"Why are we taking our tea outside when it is about to

rain?" Oona asked.

The Wizard looked up. "I suppose it is. Well, perhaps we should just get on with it. Drink up." All at once he drained his own cup and wiped at his mouth with his sleeve.

Oona glowered at the strangeness of her uncle's behavior, but she did as she was told. She had only just begun to drink when her uncle began: "Welcome to your penultimate test, Oona. The next to last. The complexity of today's challenge may seem simple at first, but it will get more difficult the longer it goes on. And how long it goes on is entirely up to you. Good luck."

Oona set her cup down, confused. "Is that all? Aren't you going to tell me what I'm supposed to do?"

The Wizard stood and looked to Samuligan. Samuligan, too, rose from his chair before reaching his long faerie fingers into his pocket and bringing out a thick metal linked chain. He tossed one end of the chain into the air, and, like a snake rising from a snake charmer's basket, it rose higher and higher until the end disappeared into the clouds.

"Well, that's quite extraordinary," Oona said.

But Samuligan paid her no mind. He laced his fingers together and cracked his bony knuckles before leaping onto the chain. The chain held his weight quite easily, and to Oona's surprise the faerie quickly climbed up the silvery links and disappeared into the ominous-looking clouds above. A moment later the chain was pulled up behind him.

"Now what?" Oona asked, but her uncle did not answer. He only stared at her expectantly, watching, waiting.

"I see," Oona said. "Not speaking, are you? Well, what about you, Deacon? What do you make of this?"

But as Deacon opened his beak to respond, the Wizard raised a hand and the only thing that came out of Deacon was a low raven caw. Uncle Alexander made another motion and Deacon flew from Oona's shoulder to the Wizard's.

Oona frowned, feeling somewhat irritated and yet excited at the same time. Here was a puzzle, and Oona loved nothing more than something to put her mind to solving.

"So, that's it, is it?" she said, and stood from the table. "I'm to figure out what to do on my own. Fine."

She did not know the spell for conjuring a chain out of thin air, but she was fairly certain that Pendulum House would know it, or something similar.

"Profundus magicus!"

The moment she linked to the house, the answer was there...the power was hers. As if she always carried it with her, Oona reached into her dress pocket and brought out the end of a piece of rope. The curious thing was that though Oona often carried a small ball of string in her pocket, along with other handy objects such as a bit of metal wire, paper and pencil, and a needle stuck in a bit of cork, she certainly had never carried around a length of rope so long as this. The house must have put it there.

She tossed the rope into the air, and as it uncoiled from her pocket, the rope weaved back and forth, tying knots and looping around itself. It ascended into the sky, creating a sturdy rope ladder, which climbed so high that, like Samuligan's chain, it, too, disappeared into the clouds above.

Oona smiled, pleased with herself at how quickly she had figured it out, and then all at once felt her stomach take a turn when she realized that she was most likely supposed to climb up the ladder after the faerie.

"Well, no sense thinking about it," she said aloud before placing one foot upon the rope ladder and grabbing hold of a higher rung with her right hand. The moment she placed her weight upon the ladder, however, the entire thing came falling back out of the sky and fell into a huge tangled heap in the street. Oona lost her balance and fell back against the gate. Her head struck one of the iron rods and the entire gate rattled on its hinges.

Rubbing at the back of her head, she pushed herself back upright and scowled at the rope...except the rope was now gone. What had gone wrong? She looked to her uncle, hoping he might point out what her flaw had been, but he only watched her, running his hand absently through his long gray beard, and Oona remembered that he was keeping quiet.

Clearly, the rope had disappeared when she had struck her head and lost her concentration. That meant that the enchanted rope existed only when she was concentrating on it.

Balancing more than one task, she thought, remembering what she had read about this particular test in the *Apprenticeship Magica*. *I'm being tested on how many things I can do at one time.*

She thought of what her uncle had said just before the test began: how the test would seem simple at first but would get more difficult as it went along. Creating the rope ladder had seemed simple enough, but climbing the ladder was, for some reason, another matter.

She looked toward the sky and scratched thoughtfully at her head. That was when she felt the first drops of rain upon her cheeks. She did her best to ignore them, along with the fact that if she didn't figure out what she was doing wrong quickly, then she would soon find herself getting wet indeed.

Why would the house let me conjure the rope but not let me climb it? she wondered, and then it occurred to her that perhaps the reason for this was because the rope ladder was not connected to something at the top that could hold her weight. The clouds were not solid, so there was no help there.

I could try to create a wooden ladder, she considered, but then realized that, same as the rope ladder, with nothing to support it at the top, it would only fall over. She also understood that the house had given the rope ladder to her because it was the right magic to use; her link with the house was still strong, and she understood this to be true.

Perhaps what I need to do is create a second spell that attaches the ladder to something in the clouds...or makes the clouds solid.

This seemed reasonable enough, though it meant concentrating on two spells at one time, something she had never done.

"Balancing more than one task," she said aloud, and once more reached into her pocket. Just as before, she brought out the end of a thick piece of rope and tossed it into the air. This time she was more aware of the magic working through her. Some of what was happening was her own magic, and some of it was the ancient magic from the house. The two intertwined, working together so perfectly that it was nearly impossible to tell where her magic stopped and the house's magic began.

The rope once more weaved its web of square-shaped patterns into the sky, disappearing into the ever-darkening clouds.

Okay, she thought, wondering how to begin the next step. *I need another spell to hold this steady.*

The thought sparked the house into an immediate response.

Gospinster's Wind!

And though she had never heard those words together in her life, they materialized in her mind as if she had known them always.

The clouds began to swirl and twist. Like an artist sculpting an enormous masterpiece in the sky, the wind formed the clouds into two massive hands that clamped hold of the end of the rope ladder, holding it steady.

Oona's head felt heavy as she concentrated as hard as she could upon both spells at the same time, splitting her mind in two. She tugged on the rope ladder. It felt strong and sturdy.

Now all I have to do is climb, she thought, which she had a feeling was going to be difficult to do while concentrating on two magical activities at the same time. She pulled herself up onto the first rung and the ladder continued to hold. So far so good, and yet as she began to climb, she became immediately aware of how difficult it was to climb even two rungs, let alone hundreds of them. The rope ladder rose hundreds of feet into the sky and she did not believe she had the strength to make the climb.

Once again the house knew precisely what to do, and it occurred to Oona that she had the solution already...except for one tiny problem: it required another piece of magic. Holding two spells within her mind at the same time was difficult enough, but could she hold three?

Looking down, she realized that she was only a few feet off the ground; if she fell now, she would not be too badly injured. She opened her mind once more to the house's magical influence and allowed the magic to enter, placing it side by side with the creation of the ladder and the cloudy hands that held it up.

It worked.

Slowly, steadily the ladder rose into the air. Oona looked down and could see the ground dropping away—her uncle, and Deacon, and soon even Pendulum House began to shrink in size—and then she looked up in amazement as the massive cloud hands pulled her up to meet them. Her heart began to pound rapidly from both excitement and fear as she clung desperately to the rope. The higher she rose, the stronger the breeze and rain felt upon her face. The thought of falling occurred to her time and time again, but so long as she did not let go she felt somehow that all would be right.

For now, she thought.

What sort of treachery Samuligan had planned within or above the clouds was another matter altogether.

As she rose into the sky and the wind played with her hair and dress, it occurred to her that, so far today, she had not uttered a single spell, which was strange because usually magic required a verbal command. She was aware that very powerful magic—that which was beyond the scope of what she had learned so far in her training—was often conjured using thoughts and feelings alone, but thus far her uncle had not taught her such advanced skills.

Yet as she linked with the house, she was linking with all of the knowledge of the Magicians of Old, who had pooled their magical know-how into the house hundreds of years ago. She began to wonder if there were any limits at all to what was possible.

She did not have time to wonder for long, however. At last the ladder pulled Oona into the graying clouds and beyond.

Her dress collected tiny pellets of water as she passed through the dense clouds. The water beaded on her eyelashes, and she blinked the drops away only to have them form again seconds later. But the ride through the clouds was brief, and before long she emerged into the bright sunlight above. There the clouds spread out beneath her like a sea of gray and white waves. It was a breathtaking sight, and for one brief moment her apprehension about what challenge Samuligan had for her vanished as she took in the awe-inspiring view.

Oona cast her gaze about, wondering where the faerie had gotten to. She spun around, only to find Samuligan waiting patiently for her inside a small rowboat. The boat bobbed upon the clouds as if floating upon rippling water.

"Climb in," Samuligan said.

Oona did as she was told, though reluctantly. Despite the beauty of her surroundings, she felt quite anxious about what might come next. The instant her foot left the ladder, the rope dropped away through the clouds and disappeared below. She peered over the edge of the boat after it, and that's when the first flash of lightning lit up the sea of clouds beneath them, followed by a rolling rumble of thunder. The sound resonated through Oona's entire body and caused the boat to rock unsteadily from side to side. Oona took her seat and clasped hold of the sides for support.

Samuligan's expression was as calm as a windless lake. "How many spells did it take?" he asked.

"Three," Oona said. "Though none of them were spoken."

"Impressive," the faerie replied. "Of course, you'll need to do better than that to wake up."

Oona's eyebrows slid closer together. "Wake up? What do you..." She trailed off, looking about her and frowning. "Is this...another illusion?"

Samuligan shook his head. "No...not really. We did illusions yesterday. But then again, what isn't an illusion?"

Oona could feel her frustration beginning to rise. "That's not very helpful at all. And if it's not an illusion, then what is it?"

"That I can't say. I'm not the one creating it."

"Creating what?"

Samuligan gestured toward the sea of clouds, which all at once looked not so much like a vast sea, but more like the rolling hills of the Dark Street Cemetery. Countless headstones poked out of the tops of the clouds, the sight of which sent goose bumps skittering up Oona's arms.

"What's this all about?" she asked.

"Again, I have no idea," the faerie replied. "Yesterday I was the one who created the illusion of Faerie. But this...this I suspect is a dream."

"A dream?" Oona said skeptically.

Samuligan shrugged. "In all of your history lessons, have you ever heard of someone being able to climb into the sky?"

Oona considered the question hard before shaking her head. "Now that you mention it...no."

"No. Not even faeries such as I possess such powers."

Oona peered around at the cemetery landscape in the sky. "I still don't understand. Then how did we manage it?"

"*I* did not manage it."

171

"What do you mean *you* didn't when I can see you clearly right—" But she stopped abruptly, a strange thought occurring to her. "You mean to say that *I* am creating this? Yesterday *you* created the illusion of Faerie, but today *I* am creating this illusion myself. But why...how—" She took in a sharp breath, remembering the cup of tea the faerie had poured for her. "You put something in my drink. In my tea. A potion."

But what potion specifically? she wondered. Every apprentice Wizard was taught that potions were breakable by their ingredients. Know the parts of the potion, and then a counterpotion or spell could be used to reverse the effects.

Samuligan only watched her with an amused expression on his long faerie face. He was not going to help. *How can I know what it's made of?* she wondered.

The question stirred Pendulum House's magic to life. A sensation like that of being squeezed through the neck of a very small bottle overcame her as her consciousness suddenly descended into her body. Her purpose was clear as the magic pulled her deeper and deeper, sniffing out the foreign substance like a bloodhound on the scent.

"Birch root...elder twig...night moss and elm. Essence of juniper and..." And something else she could not make out. An essential ingredient. She increased her awareness, opening herself even more to the house's masterful influence as she followed the magic down into her blood and the cells within. For a long moment she was no longer in the boat but swam deep within her own body, so small that she could see its workings as if they were giant machines churning their endless work: the beating of her heart, the breathing of her lungs, the miracle of life spread out before her...and yet the final ingredient of the potion eluded her.

Yet there *was* a smell. A familiar smell. Something she knew well. How strange that she could not place it. This was not plant, nor metal...it was, in fact, animal in nature. Something dark...and light...and...

Oona snapped her fingers, coming out of her magical trance. She had it. She knew the final ingredient. It was no wonder she had had such trouble identifying it because it was something so familiar that she had thought it was a part of herself and not a foreign substance at all.

"Feather of crow," Oona said. "Very similar to feather of raven."

Samuligan grinned at her from the other end of the floating boat and thumbed back his cowboy hat. "Very good."

Her link with the house told her this was a sleeping potion. "You've put me to sleep. That's why you keep saying that you aren't creating the illusion."

"Illusions created by others are easily detectable," the faerie said as he pushed himself to his feet. The boat rocked unsteadily beneath him. "But self-made illusions are the hardest to sense, and even harder to break. That is why faeries love potions. Let your enemies defeat themselves, and the act of war is so much easier. Of course, once you know what ails you, the antidote is easily made. The Magicians of Old knew this, and so do you."

Oona shook her head, confused. "But if this is all a dream that I am creating...how am I supposed to create an antidote?"

Instead of answering, Samuligan tipped his hat and smiled his mischievous grin. "You know, they say that when you fall in a dream, you always wake up just before you hit the ground."

And with that, the faerie leapt out of the boat and dropped through the clouds like a stone through water.

Oona screamed.

"Nothing to be frightened of," said a voice. Oona's scream stuck in her throat and she turned, casting about for the owner of the voice. To her surprise, she discovered a man in a long coat sitting atop one of the tombstones. Even more of a surprise was the fact that she recognized him...a man

173

who had been dead for years but who looked just as alive as he had on the last day Oona had seen him. Her mouth fell open as she stared into the clever, handsome face of her father.

Reading the startled and confused look on Oona's face, he smiled reassuringly. "Samuligan will be fine."

Oona searched for words. "But...but...you're..."

"Dead?" her father said. "Yes."

"Then how are you here?" she asked wonderingly. Her heart felt as if it were about to explode with joy at seeing him so close, and yet her mind was terribly confused. Her throat constricted as tears began to well in her eyes.

"Come now, Oona," her father said, and tapped the side of his head. His short brown hair looked just as it had on the last morning she had seen him. "How is it possible I'm here? Use your brain, little one."

Her breath hitched in her throat. "Little one" had been his nickname for her. It was something she had nearly forgotten, a fact that now made her feel quite sad. What else had she forgotten?

"Not so little anymore," Oona said. "I've grown."

He pulled his magnifying glass from his pocket and peered at her through it, making one eye look enormous. "And so you have grown. Though not quite a giant."

Oona nodded thoughtfully. "Still short, you mean."

He spun the magnifying glass playfully in his fingers. "Just right, I'd say."

Oona peered at the magnifying glass and then reached into her pocket, pulling out an exact duplicate. She held the magnifying glass that she had inherited from her father up in front of her and looked from the glass in her own hand to the one in her father's.

"How can we both be holding the same glass?" she asked.

"Think," her father said.

Oona considered the conundrum, though it did not take

her long. "You are a dream. You're not real."

"A dream, yes. Real? That's another thing altogether."

"So I brought you here. But why?"

"What do you need?"

The question struck Oona like a brick in the chest. It was unexpected and terrible—terrible because she knew the devastating answer.

"I need *you*," she said, and her voice cracked with emotion. "I need you, and Mother, and Flora to be alive."

Her father dropped his finger from the side of his head and tapped his chest. "You have us, always. Here."

Oona shook her head. "It's not enough!"

"It is more than enough," he said, and though he sounded suddenly stern, his voice never lost its edge of care.

Oona stared at him for a long moment. After a while she asked: "Can I just stay here with you?"

"That's part of the test."

"How do you mean?"

"The potion put you to sleep. Will you sleep your life away?"

Oona ran a hand through her hair, thinking. "It's why Samuligan brought me here, isn't it?"

"Samuligan didn't bring you here," her father said. "You did. And you have a purpose. That is why you won't stay."

Oona began to nod, understanding blooming like a flower in her mind's eye. "I need something. Okay, I see. What I need to know, right now, is who killed you. Can you tell me that?"

"You have all the clues," her father said, and once again peered at her through the magnifying glass. "Think. Who knew about the Rose Knot?"

Oona considered the question carefully. When she thought it through, she realized that there were only two people who knew for sure how to tie the knot.

"Isadora Iree," Oona said. "But she was only ten years

old when you were murdered, and besides, she only just learned the knot from the book."

Her father adjusted his position on the gravestone. "All right, so through a process of elimination, who does that leave?"

Oona pounded her fist on the edge of the boat, causing it to rock slowly back and forth. "That leaves only the man who wrote the book: Abraham McGillicuddy...but the book was published almost forty years ago, and according to Deacon the man never lived on Dark Street."

Oona paused for a moment, a new idea blossoming.

"But perhaps..." her father began for her.

And as if the two of them shared one mind, Oona finished: "But maybe he taught the knot to someone. Perhaps his son...or grandson. I had Deacon check the *Who's Who* specifically for an *Abraham* McGillicuddy when I should have asked if there were *any* McGillicuddys living on Dark Street at all."

"It's where I'd start," her father said.

Oona beamed at him. "Then it is where I will start, too." She looked around the boat and frowned. "Ah...just as soon as I figure out how to get down from here."

"Now that I *can* help you out with," he said, and reached into his pocket. From it he extracted a single black feather.

"Feather of crow," Oona said. "The crucial potion ingredient."

"It's a good thing you figured out what it was; otherwise, I wouldn't have found it." He held up his free hand as if about to cast a spell.

"I didn't think you knew any magic," she said.

"Oh, but I *am* the magic, don't you see?"

"I don't understand."

"You will...one day."

Her father hopped from the tombstone—which Oona now saw had his name upon it—and held his hand over the feather. His fingers began to glow orange from within, as if he held some tremendous energy.

"But wait!" Oona cried. "I don't want to leave yet. I want to talk some more...I miss you so much."

"I know, little one," was his only response before several bolts of lightning exploded from his fingertips, shooting into the feather. The explosion of thunder was like cannon fire in the sky, causing the boat to rock from side to side.

He held out the black feather, which appeared to have been unaffected by the lightning. Oona reached tentatively out and took it. For the briefest instant she felt her fingers brush against her father's—those familiar fingers that had held her as a baby and clasped her hand as she grew—and then they were gone. She took the feather in her own fingers. It felt as heavy as a mountain. The weight caused the boat to tip violently to one side and then capsize completely.

Oona shrieked, her free hand groping for purchase and scratching gouges along the edge of the boat as it tossed her into the vast openness of the sky. And then she was falling, tumbling end over end, out of control. She tumbled through the clouds—forks of lightning crisscrossing the air in a horrifying web of electricity—and then out the bottom, where all of Dark Street zoomed up to meet her. The sight was too terrifying to watch. Oona clamped her eyes shut, still gripping the inky black feather, and dropped to the street like a stone.

Chapter Thirteen

The Shoe Fly

Oona awoke with a start, sitting bolt upright in bed. She peered around, at first confused about her surroundings before realizing that someone had brought her up to her room. The sun was just beginning to rise through her window, revealing that she had been sleeping on top of her covers and was still wearing the same dress from when she had sat down at tea that afternoon.

She shook her head. No, that was not right. By the light, she could tell that it was now morning, and tea on the sidewalk had happened the previous day. She had dreamed the night away.

Something pricked her palm, and she looked down to see the black feather her father had given her clasped tightly in her right hand. Had it been a dream? If it was, then how could she still be holding the feather? She had brought it with her.

"Was it really him?" she wondered aloud.

"Hmm?" sounded a voice.

Oona looked around to find Deacon just coming awake upon her bedpost.

"Oh, you're awake," Deacon said, and stretched his

long black wings. "Your uncle said you might sleep for as long as twenty-four hours, after which time he would administer the antidote to the sleeping potion. Though he suspected that you would figure out the antidote yourself before that was necessary. It appears he was right."

"It was my father, Deacon," Oona said. She stared amazedly at the feather she had brought back with her from her dream. "He found the key ingredient and did something to it. Some powerful magic. I only figured out what the ingredients were. He's the one who broke the enchantment."

"Your father?" Deacon asked. "Are you sure you didn't just—"

"Dream it?" Oona said. "Of course I did. But it was real. Look. Here is the feather he gave to me."

Deacon shook his head from side to side. "I don't understand. Where did you get that feather? It's not one of mine."

Oona twirled it in her fingers. "No. It's similar to yours, but different. That's what made it such a difficult ingredient to figure out. The two of us are together so much that I thought it was a part of me, that it was not a foreign substance. But this is not a raven feather, it is the feather of a crow."

Deacon hopped to the bed to get a closer look. "Ah, I see, it is smaller than mine, and feather of crow has been used in many potions throughout the years. But I still don't see how you could have brought it out of your dream."

Oona opened her mouth to explain further but stopped, realizing that she did not understand it, either. She decided to change the subject.

"Deacon, what can you tell me about McGillicuddy?"

Deacon looked up at her, cocking is head sideways. "I thought we already looked into that."

"No, we didn't," Oona said, remembering the conversation she'd had with her father. She felt a sting of sadness at having spent so little time with him before having

179

to go. Her fingers clamped on the end of the feather he had handed to her. Their fingers had touched, for only the briefest of moments, but the touch, she was sure, had been real.

"I beg your pardon?" Deacon asked, clearly confused.

"You looked up *Abraham* McGillicuddy," Oona explained, "but you didn't look to see if there were any other McGillicuddys living on Dark Street. Like, perhaps, a son of his, someone who might have learned the art of knot tying from his father and then moved to Dark Street."

Deacon fell silent as he consulted the *Dark Street Who's Who*. After a moment he responded: "There are two living McGillicuddys registered as residing on Dark Street. Husband and wife. Victor and Jezebel." Deacon's eyes widened. "And Victor McGillicuddy just so happens to be the same Victor who works at the Museum of Magical History. He is the daytime watchman!"

Oona swung her feet off the bed and leapt to her feet. "Of course, Deacon. He's the one who found the night watchman the next day, and cut him free. He knocked Hackelsmith out the night before, tied him up using the knot he learned from either his father or grandfather, and stole the Faerie Carbuncle."

"According to the *Who's Who*, his family came to Dark Street when he was a boy."

"He and his wife must be the thieves!" Oona said so loudly she was nearly shouting. "Come, Deacon, we must contact Inspector White."

"But just because Victor has the same last name as the author of the knot-tying book doesn't constitute enough proof to arrest him. It doesn't even prove that he knows how to tie the knot. Remember, the knot was so complicated that he was unable to untie the night watchman in the morning, and so he had to cut the rope off."

Oona began pacing the floor, catching glimpses of her disheveled hair in the mirror as she moved. "Maybe there is no way to untie it. I saw no mention of it in the book. Or even if there is, maybe he left it there on purpose. That would be in keeping with the Rose Thieves' method of operation."

"Their *modus operandi*," Deacon said.

"Precisely," Oona said, and then a new thought occurred to her, and she began to nod. She moved to her dressing table, where she found the book of knots, and began flipping through the pages. When she came to the page she had been looking for, she pointed accusingly at the illustration, as if the knot itself had committed some heinous crime.

"I remembered seeing this when I was looking through the book," she said. "This is how we will prove that he knows these knots, Deacon."

Deacon hopped to the tabletop. "But that is not the Rose Knot."

Oona slapped the book shut. "Trust me, Deacon. This is it. But first we should send a note to police headquarters. I want Inspector White there at the museum when I confront my father's murderer."

Oona opened her bedroom window and tied the note she had written to Inspector White to Deacon's leg.

"Get this to police headquarters as quickly as possible, Deacon."

Deacon ruffled his feathers in the cool morning breeze. "I don't see why you need me to take it. Why not just send it via flame?"

Deacon was referring to the standard method of sending letters on Dark Street, which involved writing the receiving person's address upon the letter or envelope and then setting it on fire.

"Because, Deacon," Oona said impatiently, "Inspector White has told me countless times to stay out of police affairs. He might ignore my request. I need you to make sure he comes to the museum at once."

"And how am I supposed to do that?" Deacon asked.

"I'm sure you'll figure it out. Now off with you. And I'll meet you there."

Oona shooed him out the window, and Deacon took to the air on smooth black wings. A moment later Oona threw open her bedroom door, only to discover her uncle approaching from down the hall.

"Ah, you are awake," he said, looking very pleased. "I was just coming to check on you. So you figured it out, did you?"

Oona held up the black feather, which she still held tightly in her hand. "Feather of crow. That was the key ingredient."

Her uncle's expression went from pleased to confused. "Well, yes. That was the key ingredient, and you obviously counteracted it. But what is that you have there?"

Oona looked at her uncle, puzzled by the question. "It's the feather of crow. I just said."

The Wizard began to stroke ponderously at his beard. "You brought it physically back with you?"

"Wasn't that supposed to happen?" she asked.

"I won't lie—it is quite extraordinary, don't you think? You carried it out of a dream."

"My father gave it to me."

The Wizard's bushy white eyebrows shot up. "Bradford? You saw him?"

Oona nodded. "Just after Samuligan jumped out of the boat. Where is Samuligan anyway? Is he all right?"

"I am perfectly fine," the faerie said, emerging from the shadow of a nearby doorway. "I see you brought back a souvenir." Samuligan pointed a long finger at the black feather.

"I did," Oona said, and as much as she wished to know more about why she had been able to bring the feather back with her, she was also boiling inside with anticipation for catching her father's killer. "But that's not important right now. We need to get to the museum. Samuligan, can you fetch the carriage?"

"At once," he said, and he was gone, moving down the hallway with uncanny speed and disappearing down the stairs.

"Is everything all right?" the Wizard asked.

Oona opened her mouth, meaning to tell her uncle precisely what she had figured out, but something stopped her. A thought occurred to her, a sense that if her uncle knew what she was planning on doing, then he would never allow her to go. But she had to go. She had to be there when her father's killer was finally exposed. It was she, after all, who had figured out who had done it, and she was determined to see the case through to its end.

"I just have some business to attend to at the museum," Oona said.

"May I see it?" the Wizard asked. "The feather."

Oona felt the knot in her stomach tighten. She wanted to get a move on...but knew she should do as her uncle asked. She handed the feather over.

For a long moment her uncle did not say anything, just stared at the feather with a rather wistful expression on his face. At last he said: "Lynette."

Oona shook her head. "I beg pardon."

Her uncle cleared his throat. "Lynette Abshire. That was her name. The woman I was in love with."

Oona's mouth dropped open, remembering the question she had asked him in the park and surprised that he was now answering it. She was not certain how to respond, and was also a bit frustrated that he would choose now of all times to open up. And yet, she could not hold back her curiosity.

"What happened to her?" she asked, partly dreading what the answer might be.

The Wizard turned his gaze from the feather to Oona, almost as if he were surprised to see her there, and Oona wondered if perhaps the feather had some power that was affecting him. The slight sadness that always rested just behind his eyes suddenly looked more pronounced than ever.

"Oh, she is not dead, if that is what you are thinking," the Wizard replied. "She is a happily married woman with several grown children of her own. It's just that...well, you see, I had a choice. Give up my apprenticeship to Wizard Flirtensnickle and be with her, or follow my ambition to become the next Wizard."

Oona placed a hand to her mouth. "But why? Why did you have to make a choice? I don't understand."

"Because Lynette whished to have a simple life...not one that involved the complexities of the Wizard's life. She told me so when we first began our courtship. I was so enamored with everything about her...her beauty, the sound of her voice, her bright and hopeful personality, and most especially the way she looked at me, which made me feel as if I were the most special young man on all of Dark Street. I knew that there were other male suitors eager to charm her...and so I led her on, letting her believe that I was going to give up the apprenticeship. I half believed it myself. But finally, when it came time for me to make a decision...I chose the Wizardship." He paused, staring at the feather. "I don't regret it."

His words sounded sincere, but Oona couldn't help but wonder if they were completely true. His eyes seemed to suggest otherwise.

The Wizard shook his head and handed the feather back to Oona. "I don't know why I'm telling you all of this. I'm sure you are uninterested in an ancient heartbreak, and I can tell you are in a hurry. Won't you tell me what you are up to?"

Oona swallowed hard. Her uncle could not have been more wrong about her interest in his story. She would have loved to hear more, but he was right, and she was in a hurry.

"It's a surprise," she said.

"A surprise?" her uncle asked. "Now I'm curious."

"You'll see," Oona said, and then turned down the hall. Before she got very far, however, she turned back. "I'm sorry, Uncle...that she broke your heart."

The Wizard shook his head. "Oh, Lynette did not break my heart...*I* did. But alas, a broken heart is not the worst thing in the world. There are those who might go their entire lives having never been truly in love. It is they whom I feel the most compassion for. Anyway, don't forget, we have your final battle test today."

Oona's head gave a little jerk in surprise. "But Deacon said you were going to let me sleep for twenty-four hours."

"I was, but tradition dictates that the final challenge take place on the same day you awaken from the dream test. Had I administered the antidote tomorrow, then tomorrow would have been the day."

"I see," Oona said, before once again starting down the hall. She felt bad for rushing off just when her uncle was being so vulnerable, but she did not think it could be helped. Remembering the loving face of her father in her dream, she simply could not wait any longer to bring his killers to justice.

"What time do I need to be back?" she called back to her uncle.

"We're meeting here at twelve noon to head to the cemetery."

Again she stopped in her tracks.

"The cemetery?" she asked, thinking of the dream cemetery in the clouds.

"Yes. It will take us a while to get there by carriage, so don't be late. We don't want to still be there after sunset."

The Wizard was referring to the fact that, after sunset, the spirits of the dead came alive in the night and haunted the cemetery grounds, along with a regiment of poltergeists who guarded the graveyard entrance, preventing any ghosts or living humans from passing.

Oona's throat had suddenly gone dry, and she felt her hands go tingly with nerves, not so much from the thought of ghosts—though the idea was quite disturbing in and of itself—but from something more personal. She thought of the graves of her mother, and sister, and father in the Crate family plot...of how she had not visited them since the day of their funerals over three years ago.

"Are you sure you're all right?" the Wizard asked. "You look pale."

Oona did her best to shake the feeling off.

"I'll be here," she said, and quickly began descending the stairs. She glanced at the clock on the wall as she crossed the open antechamber toward the front door. The hour hand pointed to ten o'clock. There was no time to waste.

"Perfect timing," Oona said.

She peered out the carriage window as Samuligan pulled the horse to a stop in front of the museum. Outside, Oona could see Inspector White climbing the steps and waiving his hands in the air in an attempt to shoo Deacon away. The raven was currently swooping about the inspector's head, herding him toward the museum entrance.

Several steps behind them, a uniformed police constable followed, grinning ear to ear and watching the whole scene with open amusement.

Oona stepped from the carriage and hurried up the stone steps after them, the book of knots tucked beneath one arm.

"There you are, Miss Crate!" the inspector howled at her. The two of them reached the top step together, and the inspector took one last swipe at Deacon before the raven landed composedly upon Oona's shoulder.

"Excellent work, Deacon," Oona said.

"I did my best," Deacon replied, and he puffed out his chest, clearly proud of himself.

The inspector arrowed a finger at her. "What is the meaning of all of this? That bird of yours nearly pecked me to death!"

Oona shook her head. "I doubt that, Inspector. He was only making sure you got here in time to capture a deadly criminal."

"What are you talking about?" the inspector asked.

"Follow me, and all will be revealed," Oona said, and pulled open the thick wooden museum door.

And there he was, the daytime watchman, Victor McGillicuddy. He stood where he always did, beside the museum registry, which all visitors to the museum were required to sign. Oona had half expected him not to be there—that he would have somehow known they were coming for him and that he would have made a run for it. But no, there he stood, bold as could be, watching them approach as if he had nothing in the world to hide.

Oona's hands began to sweat, despite the coolness of the entryway. She felt nervous and angry, and yet she did not feel nearly as frightened as she thought she ought to. She was confronting a killer, after all: the man who had murdered one of the most important people in Oona's life, the one who had robbed her of anything close to a normal existence. Looking at the man now, it was hard to believe that he was capable of stealing anything, let alone of murder. But Oona supposed that such people were able to hide their secrets deep within their dark well of lies.

"Mr. McGillicuddy," Oona said. She came to a stop beside the registry, Deacon puffing himself up menacingly upon her shoulder.

Inspector White and the constable halted just behind her.

187

Victor McGillicuddy looked at the entourage with nothing more than mild curiosity. Surely, he must know that they were on to him. How the man could remain so cool, Oona was not sure.

"Yes," the guard said. "Got some more questions for me, do you?" He looked expectedly from Oona to the inspector.

The inspector crossed his arms and looked sternly at Oona. "Yes, Miss Crate. Why *are* we here?"

Oona opened the book of knots and flipped to the page containing the Rose Knot. "See this, Inspector? Do you recognize it?"

The inspector's dark eyebrows came nearly together as he leaned forward to examine the illustration. "I believe I have seen it somewhere before."

Oona's face went red as she forced herself to suppress her anger. "Of course you have seen it before. It is the knot that the thieves used to tie up the night watchman. It is the signature of the infamous Rose Thieves. The same thieves who murdered my father over three years ago."

Oona glanced at Victor McGillicuddy, hoping to discover signs of guilt, but the museum guard appeared only curious. Her conviction that he was the culprit began to waver.

She continued: "The person who wrote this book almost forty years ago is the inventor of the Rose Knot. He is also the inventor of this knot as well." She flipped the book several pages back to a knot named the Shoe Fly. "This is a sophisticated way of tying a shoe."

The inspector and the constable let out a collective "Oooooh" sound. The illustration showed a shoelace crisscrossing in a deceptively simple pattern that resembled a double-winged dragonfly.

"That's quite beautiful," Inspector White said. "I've never seen anyone tie their shoes like that before. It's a work of art."

"I agree," Oona said. "And it stands to reason that if the author of this book taught this Shoe Fly Knot to someone, then he might have also taught the Rose Knot to him."

"What are you getting at Miss Crate?" the inspector snapped.

Oona raised an eyebrow at the museum guard, staring at him hard. "Would you please raise your pant leg, Mr. McGillicuddy? So that we might see how your shoe is tied."

"I beg your pardon?" the guard asked, looking quite surprised by the request.

Oona could feel her heart begin to quicken. This was the moment of revelation. "If you have nothing to hide, Mr. McGillicuddy, please show us your shoelaces."

The guard looked to Inspector White, whose mouth had pulled into a tight line. He looked quite irritated with the entire affair, but twirled his finger in a let's-get-this-over-with gesture.

The guard shrugged, and then hiked the bottom of his trouser leg up, exposing his shiny black shoes. Oona pointed at the place where the string came together in a knot and opened her mouth to utter a triumphant "*Aha!*"...but the sound stuck in her throat.

The guard's shoelaces were not tied in any extraordinary way. They looked just like anybody else's laces. Oona's face flushed with embarrassment.

"Are you satisfied, Miss Crate?" the inspector asked.

Oona threw her hands to her hips. "So maybe he doesn't use the Shoe Fly Knot to tie his shoes. That doesn't mean he doesn't know the Rose Knot." Oona flipped the book to the front cover. "The author of this book is Abraham McGillicuddy, and it seems highly suspicious to me that—"

"That's my grandfather's name!" the guard blurted out.

Oona took in a sharp breath. "So you admit it."

"Of course I do," he said plainly. "But I didn't know he had published a book. Can I see that?"

189

Oona reluctantly handed the book over.

The guard began flipping through the pages, his expression growing more and more thoughtful. "Grandfather passed away in New York, just before my family moved to Dark Street, back when I was a kid. And now that I think of it, he did have a hobby that had to do with knots...except he never taught me any of them. Not a very nice man, my grandfather. Didn't care for me much, as I remember. But he loved my older sister, Abigail, he did. Treated her like a little princess."

"Your sister?" Oona asked, surprised. She looked at Deacon, wondering why the name Abigail McGillicuddy had not appeared in the *Who's Who*.

Before she could inquire, Victor continued: "I think he taught Abigail quite a few of his knots, come to think of it, but she never showed 'em to me. Then again, I never was much interested in that sort of thing, and we never were very close, she being some nine years older than me. Plus, she got married to that shady character Denis Carlyle. My wife insisted I stop inviting them to dinner because things kept disappearing. Haven't seen either of them in years."

"Carlyle?" Oona said, and looked alarmingly at Deacon. "Is that..." She didn't even wish to finish the sentence.

Deacon appeared thoughtful as he accessed his reference materials. After a pause, he said: "Oh, dear. Had we inquired further into the *Dark Street Who's Who*, we would have seen the connection. But we stopped at the name McGillicuddy. Abigail McGillicuddy changed her last name when she got married to Denis Carlyle—a man with quite a checkered past—and became Abigail Carlyle...and she is currently the housemaid at Pendulum House."

Oona's heart sank.

Chapter Fourteen

The Final Battle Test

Oona shoved through the front door to Pendulum House so forcefully that the door banged against the inside wall, causing Deacon to jump on her shoulder. Inspector White and the police constable followed her in, with Samuligan bringing up the rear.

"Where is she?" Oona asked. She peered around the entryway as if expecting to find the maid standing there, waiting for them. But the entryway and the round antechamber beyond stood empty.

"Tell me again why we are searching for your housemaid," the inspector said incredulously.

Oona whirled around. "Because, Inspector, she is the only person we know for sure who would know how to tie the Rose Knot—besides Isadora Iree, that is, but Isadora is too young to have murdered my father three years ago. Whoever did it was in league with Red Martin. He told me so. As you know, my father had been trying to catch the Rose Thieves when he was killed. They tied that very knot to the murder weapon, the gun, and left it behind. It was their signature. And it's the same knot used on the night watchman at the museum on Monday night."

"And you want me to arrest her based solely on the fact that she might know how to tie a knot?" the inspector asked.

"A *unique* knot, Inspector...but what I suggest you do is take Mrs. Carlyle back to her home and search it for the missing Faerie Carbuncle. That should prove she is one of the Rose Thieves." Oona turned back to the antechamber, where several hallways branched off in different directions. "Samuligan, can you fetch Mrs. Carlyle for us? Samuligan?"

She looked around but did not see the faerie anywhere. "Where did he get to?"

"I have already searched for her. She is not here," said the faerie, who, to Oona's surprise, entered the antechamber from the hallway that led to the library.

"That was quick," Oona said, quite impressed, though she knew she should not have been. The faerie was almost a part of the house and had a knack for appearing in nearly any room to which he was summoned at the drop of a hat.

"But that is not all," Samuligan continued. "There is a book missing from the library. A very old book of spells."

"A book of spells?" Deacon asked. "Are you sure?"

"I know that library like the back of my hand," Samuligan said. He held up his hand, which presently displayed an intricate tattooed map of the library's forest of books. "I knew the book was missing the moment I entered."

Oona shook her head, confused. "You think Mrs. Carlyle took it? But what would she want with..." She trailed off as the answer came to her. It was a terrible answer, one that she wished were not true.

"Oona? What's going on here?" came the voice of the Wizard. He was crossing the antechamber toward them.

"It's Mrs. Carlyle," Oona said. "She is one of the Rose Thieves."

The Wizard stopped in his tracks. "The Rose Thieves? The ones responsible for your father's death? Bradford's murderers?"

Hearing her uncle say it out loud all at once made her want to burst into tears, and it occurred to her that she had been fighting back her emotions ever since approaching the museum guard. She swallowed hard and forced herself to keep her emotions in check for as long as possible.

"One and the same," she said. "Surely the other Rose Thief must be her husband, Denis Carlyle...the man she said she met when she was around my age."

And suddenly Oona felt a sense of betrayal like she had never felt before. She had confided in Mrs. Carlyle, told her about Adler, and even looked up to her for her thoughts on women's rights. It was simply wretched.

Oona cleared her throat before continuing: "They stole the Faerie Carbuncle from the museum, and now she has stolen a book of ancient spells from the Pendulum House library. Most likely, she's been looking for the spell that is required to activate the carbuncle's enchantment."

The Wizard ran a thoughtful hand down his beard. "That's why I always found her cleaning the library. I just thought she was being thorough."

Oona began to nod, understanding coming too late. "It's true. I almost always found her there as well. She was pretending to clean the shelves when what she was really up to was looking for a book that contained the spell she would need to activate the Faerie Carbuncle which would—"

"Give her faerielike powers," Deacon finished.

"I'll bet that's why she applied for the housemaid position in the first place," Oona said. "She's been here only a month. I'll bet she knew that she and her husband were going to try to steal the carbuncle before she even applied. It was planned the whole time, but the Pendulum House library was so disorganized." Oona looked to Samuligan, who raised a questioning eyebrow at her. "That is to say, so *seemingly* disorganized that it took her a month to find what she was looking for. But now she's found it."

"We don't know that for sure," said the Wizard.

"But it's likely," Oona said. "Why else would she steal the book? We must go to Mrs. Carlyle's home and confront her, this instant...before she gets a chance to use the spell."

"Hold on, Oona," her uncle said. "If what you are hypothesizing is true, then this is a matter for the police."

"That is correct," said Inspector White, though to Oona's ears he sounded less than fully confident.

Oona crossed her arms. "But she has stolen a magical artifact and a magical book, which together could be disastrously dangerous. I think that puts it in our magical jurisdiction."

"You mean to say *my* jurisdiction, Oona, not yours," her uncle said, his tone quite stern. "You are not the Wizard yet, and I will decide what actions we take." He glanced at the clock on the wall. "It's nearly noon now, and we have your final battle test in the cemetery to attend to. We mustn't start too late, because as we know, the cemetery is no place to be after sunset. Oh, and you'll be needing this, once more."

He pulled Oswald's wand from his pocket and handed it to Oona. She looked at it in her own hand for a moment and then shook her head.

"But, Uncle, surely—"

The Wizard held up his hand. "That is my final word on this, Oona. We'll leave it to Inspector White to track her down."

Inspector White stuck his thumbs into the waistband of his trousers and puffed out his chest, as if he could not have been prouder. "You can count on me. Constable Mormont and I will track them down. In fact, I know just where to begin."

"Where is that?" Oona asked skeptically.

"Oh, we have our ways, Miss Crate. Never fear...Inspector White is on the case."

Oona could only shake her head. Her insides twisted with anxiety. Surely, the inspector would do something stupid and the Carlyles would get away. But it seemed she had no choice.

The cemetery was located at the southernmost end of the street, close to the Glass Gates. A six-mile journey from Pendulum House, the carriage ride was a long one. It gave Oona time to brood.

She couldn't believe how stupid she had been for befriending the very person who was responsible for her father's death. The maid had seemed so caring and interested in Oona's life, and yet it seemed now that it had been a masterful act, every conversation a complete fraud. Oona felt foolish for having shared her hopes and dreams with someone she had thought a friend. A true female companion.

Oona wondered if Mrs. Carlyle's interest in the women's rights movement had been a sham as well. The thought reminded her of what day it was.

"Oh, I nearly forgot," she said, looking at her uncle, who sat beside her in the carriage. "It's voting day."

The Wizard's beard wiggled and swayed with every bump in the street. He nodded. "It is. I voted early this morning at the central Dark Street precinct. I wanted to beat the crowds. But look, you can see some of the action for yourself. We're coming up on City Hall."

Oona peered out the window and saw a line of people stretching down the street that led to the front entrance of City Hall, a reddish, square-shaped building that had always looked to Oona as if someone had dropped an enormous brick from the sky. It was the only building on Dark Street that had perfectly straight walls, with Roman columns out front and a pair of carved stone griffons guarding the entrance.

The line of people stretched up the street for as far as

Oona could see.

"They're all voting?" Oona asked.

"The publicity in yesterday's paper seems to have caused a larger-than-usual turnout," the Wizard said.

"You mean this isn't normal?"

The Wizard shook his head, but it was Deacon who answered from his perch on the windowsill. "Council elections are held every two years, and in the past ten years, the average number of voters in each election has totaled fewer than one thousand."

"Is that all?" Oona asked, flabbergasted. "But there are tens of thousands of people living on Dark Street."

Presently, they pulled up even with City Hall, where the line of voters entered the building. Something struck the carriage so forcefully that Oona was flung out of her seat. Deacon let out a sharp cry and took to the air as the entire riding compartment tipped sideways and slammed down in the middle of the street.

Oona landed on top of her uncle with a crunching sound.

She took in a startled breath, shaking her head and blinking confusedly. "Uncle Alexander?" Oona asked wearily. "Are you all right?"

No response.

Outside the carriage, along with the shouts of people, she thought she heard the sounds of barking dogs. Oona scrambled to her left, just now realizing that the carriage was lying on its side. She looked at the Wizard and saw that the large sleeve of his robe was covering his face. He wasn't moving.

"Uncle?" she asked again, and she could hear the panic in her own voice. She pulled the sleeve of his robe away and exposed his face. A trickle of blood ran down the side of his head and into his beard. His eyes were closed, and she could not tell if he was breathing. Her panic swelled like some monstrous creature inside of her, and she thought for a moment that she might faint.

And then a voice spoke from above her. "I don't think you'll be needing this."

Oona looked up and her heart leapt into her throat. It was Mrs. Carlyle, who reached down through the open window and groped for something. Oona didn't know what the woman was trying to get at, but a sense of fierce rage like she had never experienced before dropped over her.

"You did this," Oona said, and she leapt at the woman's arm, her fingers like claws.

But Mrs. Carlyle raised a hand in a halting gesture, and Oona froze in midmotion. She couldn't move. She'd been somehow paralyzed. Outside the carriage, the sound of snarling dogs continued to fill the street, and for the first time Oona wondered where Samuligan was.

"I'll just be taking this and be on my way," the maid said, and snapped her fingers. Something from near where Oona had landed flew into Mrs. Carlyle's hand. Still dazed from the crash, it took Oona an instant to focus on what it was. And then she saw it: Oswald's wand.

"Thanks so much for letting me know that you use this during your tests. As you know, my boss, Red Martin, has been wanting it for some time," Mrs. Carlyle said, and Oona could see a red gem hanging from a fine gold chain around her neck. The carbuncle! Clearly, the maid had found the spell she needed to activate the gem's magic, and she now wielded extraordinary powers.

"Samuligan!" Oona shouted, surprised that she could speak at all. It seemed that whatever enchantment Mrs. Carlyle had used to freeze Oona in place had failed to paralyze her mouth.

Mrs. Carlyle looked up and over her shoulder toward something outside the carriage. "I believe your faerie servant has his hands full at the moment. You know, I never did like him."

"*Profundus mag—*" Oona began, in an attempt to link

her magic with Pendulum House, but Mrs. Carlyle pinched her fingers together and the motion caused Oona's lips to clamp shut. Even more extraordinary was that her thought of the word was frozen as well. She was unable even to think the spell.

"Ah, ah, ah. No spells from you, missy," Mrs. Carlyle said admonishingly. She considered Oona for a moment. "It's too bad you're such a powerful magician, Miss Crate; otherwise, I might be able to let you live. But knowing you, you'll try to come after me, just like your father." She aimed the wand at Oona. "That wouldn't be—"

But this time it was Mrs. Carlyle who was cut short. She cried out in pain as black wings fluttered wildly above her head and Deacon dug his talons into the maid's hair. The maid opened her hand in an attempt to grab at the bird, in the process releasing Oona from the silencing spell.

"*Profundus magicus!*" Oona cried, and just as it had in her battle tests, the incantation linked her own magic with the vast stores of magic in Pendulum House.

"*Kraken-mooris!*" The words came to her of their own accord, an ancient spell that wound itself around her own body and then quickly expanded outward, exploding Mrs. Carlyle's paralyzing spell in a burst of blue and white light. Oona was free.

"Get off me, bird!" Mrs. Carlyle howled from the side of the carriage, and raised Oswald's wand over her head. Oona witnessed another flash of light—this one a bolt of lightning that shot from the tip of the wand—which came within centimeters of hitting one of Deacon's wildly flapping wings. He must have felt the closeness of it because he abruptly untangled himself from the maid's hair and took to the sky, cawing his low raven's cry before turning in the air and diving straight for the woman's head. She raised the wand for a second attack, but she was too slow and was forced to duck away from the raven's snapping beak.

The sudden movement must have unbalanced her

because Oona watched as the maid tumbled over the side of the carriage and out of view. With a surprising surge of strength, Oona leapt upward and pulled herself through the open carriage window, where she was finally able to see what was happening outside. She stood atop the carriage.

To her right, she discovered Samuligan standing in the middle of a circle of vicious wild dogs. A translucent wall of mist—Oona assumed it had been cast by the faerie servant—surrounded Samuligan, and was all that kept the dogs at bay.

The dogs glowed slightly, as if their coats had been sprinkled with golden dust, and several of them had what appeared to be a set of wicked-looking wings made of bones that grew from their shoulder blades. One of the dogs twisted around just enough for Oona to get a glimpse of its eyes, which glowed red like burning coals.

Samuligan made a motion—pushing the wall of mist away—and then attempted to leap high over the dogs. To Oona's horror, several of the glowing hounds rose into the air, flapping their hideous bonelike wings, their jaws snapping and dripping with drool. Samuligan fell quickly back and was forced once again to conjure the wall of mist between the maniacal dogs and himself.

The line of pedestrians in front of City Hall backed up against the wall but did not disperse. It seemed they were enthralled by the extraordinary display of magic happening in the street.

"Look out!" Deacon cried.

Oona whirled around just in time to see Mrs. Carlyle raising Oswald's wand in Oona's direction. Oona leapt from the side of the toppled carriage to the street, just managing to avoid a burst of lightning. She hit the ground hard, sending stinging needles through her feet and legs as the lightning bolt struck one of the carriage wheels. The wheel tore free of the carriage and exploded in a fiery burst of chunks and splinters. The smell of singed wood filled the air.

Oona raised one hand over her head to shield herself

from the falling debris while shoving her other hand into her pocket. A second later she was holding her father's magnifying glass and aiming it in the direction she had last seen Mrs. Carlyle, but the maid was suddenly gone. Oona scanned the seen of the wreckage, but didn't see her anywhere.

"Show yourself!" Oona shouted.

Deacon, who soared high overhead, called down to her: "She's around the other side of the carriage." He let out a sharp croak as a bolt of lightning shot toward him, nearly singeing his tail feathers and sending him flying down the street for refuge.

Oona bolted around the side of the overturned carriage, a devastating question chasing her every step: Was her uncle dead, or just unconscious? There had been no time to check properly. Her throat seemed to tighten as the image of the blood trickling down the side of his head filled her thoughts.

She came to a stop at the edge of the carriage, fearing that if she stepped around, Mrs. Carlyle would be waiting for her. Her father's magnifying glass was no match for the accuracy of Oswald's wand, yet despite the disadvantage, she knew that she had to bring the wicked woman down. Not just because Mrs. Carlyle was responsible for her father's death, but because, with such incredible powers at the maid's disposal, Oona didn't think anyone was safe. She could only hope that her own skills as a magician would be enough to tip the scales in her favor.

And besides, Oona thought, *I've got the power of Pendulum House behind me, with or without Oswald's wand.*

Oona looked to the sky and opened her mouth to call to Deacon, meaning to ask if it was safe to step around the corner, when it occurred to her that she did not need to do this. Instead, she closed her eyes and whispered: *"Connect."*

The instant she shut her eyes, she no longer saw through her own eyes but through those of Deacon. He was soaring back in her direction, high above the line of pedestrians on the sidewalk. From this vantage point she could see everything.

At first she was only confused, because Mrs. Carlyle was not where Oona expected her to be. But a second later, when Deacon's eyes focused in on the woman, Oona's heart hammered hard in her chest. The maid had snuck all the way around the carriage and was coming up behind Oona.

Oona's eyes flew open and she whirled around just as several pedestrians cried out warnings. Oona thought she heard Deacon's own warning from above as she raised her magnifying glass like a shield. In that same instant, Mrs. Carlyle leapt from around the side of the carriage, wand aimed at Oona.

A sizzling bolt of white light shot from the end of the wand and collided with Oona's magnifying glass. The glass seemed to expand and glow white-hot all at the same time. And then it exploded in her hand. She stumbled back, blinded by the enormous flash. She only just managed to stay on her feet, but her hand was now empty, the magnifying glass gone, blown into a million fragments all over the street.

Oona blinked frantically and cringed, expecting a second attack at any moment to finish her off now that she was defenseless. But when her eyes finally cleared, she saw that it was no longer Mrs. Carlyle standing before her but an enormous creature with the body of a man and the head of a bull. In its thick, muscle-knotted hands it brandished a hammer that looked as if it might weigh twice Oona's body weight.

Oona's breath caught in her throat.

It's a minotaur, she thought, remembering the illustration she had seen in *Mortenstine's Monstrous Conspectus*. More than the illustration, however, she remembered telling Mrs. Carlyle about how she, Oona, had once read the *Monstrous Conspectus* before bed, and then suffered a terrifying dream about the minotaur...only there was something off about this beast who stood before her now. It was different than the one she had dreamed about all those years ago, Oona felt sure of it.

Or perhaps it was not that there was something different about the creature, but that there was something that had changed in Oona. It did not take long for her to figure it out.

It's an illusion, she thought, remembering her recent visit to the Faerie Royal Court. *It looks real, but it's not.*

The knowledge, however, did not stop her screaming as the monstrous beast suddenly raised its enormous war hammer above its head and ran at her. But the scream transformed as it exited her mouth, the tone pulling in and refining itself into one continuous note of sublime harmony with each of Oona's senses. The note carried out long, and powerful, and eerily beautiful. Her tone rattled the nearby windows and caused the hammer to explode in the minotaur's hand, just as her magnifying glass had exploded in hers.

And just like that, the illusion was broken. Oona blinked her eyes clear, only to find herself once again staring into the face of the woman she had so naively befriended. The minotaur was gone, and Mrs. Carlyle's face pulled into a mask of rage.

"Think you're clever, eh?" the maid taunted.

"I know I am," Oona said, and the words came out sounding more confident than she felt.

The maid looked pityingly at her. "Too clever for your own good, that is. Just like your father. He was another one who couldn't leave well enough alone. I guess it runs in the family. But I suppose I can put an end to that right now."

The maid once again leveled Oswald's wand, and Oona stepped back against the toppled carriage. Something poked her in the leg...something in her pocket.

"I trusted you," Oona said.

Again the maid displayed that look of pity. "Bad idea."

202

Oona inched her hand into her pocket. "You wouldn't dare kill me in front of all of these people."

Now Mrs. Carlyle just looked amused. "Oh, really? You think just because *you* can break a powerful illusion that these nonmagical people can as well? No, they will see whatever I wish for them to see: a sunny day where nothing extraordinary happened on the street at all. They'll forget everything they saw here today, and we'll all live happily ever after. Well, except for you...and your uncle. Now that I have this," she pinched the carbuncle between the fingers of her free hand, "who's going to challenge me? Certainly not you and your uncle. I'm going to make sure of that."

Oona raised an eyebrow. "You're forgetting about someone."

The maid's mouth pulled into a tight disbelieving line. "And who is that?"

"Samuligan the Fay," Oona said matter-of-factly.

"Oh, I think those hellhounds I summoned will take good care of him," the maid said confidently.

"I wouldn't be too sure of that," Oona said.

"Neither would I," said Samuligan.

The maid turned abruptly in the direction of the voice, only to discover the faerie servant standing right behind her, his wild grin lighting up his face like a bad dream. Behind him, the hellhounds were all conveniently distracted by a giant leg of lamb that the faerie had conjured and set them fighting over. As the maid had been talking, Oona had watched Samuligan approach on feet as quiet as a breeze.

Mrs. Carlyle let out a shriek of surprise as Samuligan grabbed her hand, but before he could pry the wand from her grasp, the maid managed one last spell. It shot like a bullet straight at Oona. Had she not chosen that precise moment to pull the feather from her pocket, it would surely have struck her straight in the chest. But the spell collided with the feather of crow, which seemed to absorb the full impact of the fiery bolt of magic like a sponge. The black feather began to glow, turning first orange, and then red, and finally completely white.

Oona held on with all of her strength, and yet at the same time it seemed that she could not have let go if she had tried. For several long seconds, the connection between Oswald's wand and the feather would not break, as if the feather were drawing every last bit of magic from the wand into itself. Oona could see Samuligan trying to wrestle the wand from the maid's grip, but Oona had a feeling that in that moment Mrs. Carlyle, like Oona herself, was helpless to hold the terrible link between wand and feather.

And when at last the spell broke, it came with a tremendous cracking sound, like the sound of an entire forest of trees being snapped in half all at the same time. Oona stumbled back against the carriage, and Mrs. Carlyle suddenly ceased her struggle with Samuligan. The maid peered at the broken object in her hand. Only half of the wand remained in her grip. The other half lay upon the ground like a broken pencil.

"You...you destroyed it," Mrs. Carlyle said, her voice filled with astonishment.

Oona was quite shocked as well, and no sooner had the maid spoken than the two halves of the wand began to disintegrate before their eyes, leaving Mrs. Carlyle with nothing but a handful of dust.

Samuligan took advantage of the distraction and deftly took hold of the gem hanging around Mrs. Carlyle's neck. He yanked. The fine gold chain snapped as the faerie stepped away, holding the precious object in his tightly closed fist and leaving the maid powerless.

Mrs. Carlyle realized too late what was happening and screamed. "No! You give that back!"

"I think not," said a familiar voice, and Oona spun around. Her uncle's head stuck out of the open window of the toppled carriage.

"Uncle, you're all right!" Oona said, and a sense of

relief flooded her so forcefully she felt her knees wobble beneath her. She placed a hand upon the carriage for support.

The Wizard touched the side of his head, which was tacky with blood. "Well, alive, anyway."

Oona looked down at the feather in her hand, and then turned to Mrs. Carlyle. "So, it was all a lie, wasn't it? You were never a true friend. All you cared about was finding the book of spells. You knew from the moment Uncle Alexander hired you last month that you were planning on stealing the carbuncle...and you knew that the Pendulum House library was the only place to find the spell you needed."

For a long moment, Mrs. Carlyle looked as if she were going to deny Oona's allegation, but then she shrugged and said: "The truth is, Mr. Carlyle and I have not needed to steal anything for a very long time...three years, in fact...but eventually money got tight, so we came up with the plan to steal the carbuncle and find the spell that would give us faerielike powers."

"And with those powers, you could become unstoppable thieves," Oona said. She felt a tugging sensation in her gut, as if someone had tied her insides into knots. A terrible realization came to her, and when she spoke, the tremble in her voice nearly choked her up completely. "You said you have not needed to steal anything for three years. That's because...because when you murdered my father, Red Martin paid you enough money to last you for three years."

Mrs. Carlyle's face screwed up into a harsh scowl. "Longer, actually...but my stupid husband gambled more than half of the money away." And then the maid's eyes widened at Oona as she realized what she had just admitted.

Oona's own eyes narrowed. "And where is Denis Carlyle, your husband, anyway? The man you met when you were my age."

"He is here," said a high, irritating voice.

Oona turned just in time to find Inspector White jumping down from the passenger seat of a police carriage.

The police constable sat rigidly on the driver's seat. Through the iron bars of the carriage window, Oona glimpsed the face of a man she had seen before, but could not place from where.

"There's that scoundrel!" called yet another voice. To Oona's surprise, it was John David Moon, who stepped out of the surrounding crowd, along with Molly Morgana Moon.

"I beg your pardon?" asked the inspector.

Mr. Moon pointed at the man behind the bars of the police carriage. "That man, Denis Carlyle, is responsible for the riot at the rally."

It suddenly occurred to Oona where she had seen Denis Carlyle before. He was the man who had been arguing with John David Moon just before the riot broke out.

"That scallywag came to me the night before the rally," Mr. Moon continued. He pointed an accusing finger at Mrs. Carlyle. "Along with his wife. They tried to convince me to stage a riot at the rally. They said it would be good publicity, especially if the people who started the riot were holding signs in support of Tobias Fink. People would think Fink was behind it and vote against him."

Molly Morgana Moon took in a sharp breath. "John! You never told me about this."

He looked at his wife, somewhat abashed. "I didn't want to worry you. You had too much to think about already, what with all of the fund-raising you've been doing. And besides, I told them such a stunt was out of the question. I knew people might get hurt, and I explained that we would never stoop to such treachery. But the next day, Denis Carlyle showed up at the rally and told me that the riot was going to happen whether we liked it or not. I argued with him to put a stop to it, but it was too late. The mob was already there."

Oona peered hard at Mr. Moon. "So you knew who was behind it, and you said nothing afterward?"

John David Moon's face went rose red as he realized

what he had just revealed. "Well, it had already happened...so, yes, I remained quiet. If the newspaper found out that I had known about it, they could easily have turned the story against us, even though we did nothing wrong. Newspapers have a way of doing that. I had to think of the campaign, so I said nothing. But then I saw him there in the police wagon and...well, I figured I might as well come forward with what I knew."

Deacon fluttered down to Oona shoulder and cawed disapprovingly at Mr. Moon. "You mean because you felt guilty for hiding information? Or because you were afraid of what Denis Carlyle might tell the police now that he was already arrested?"

"Or," Oona added thoughtfully, "perhaps he knew it was too late for the papers to print a story before voting is finished."

Mr. Moon stiffened, his words coming out sharp and clipped. "I did nothing wrong. I did my best to stop the riot."

Oona shook her head, unsure of how she felt about this. She looked at Molly Morgana Moon, wondering what she thought. For a long moment Mrs. Moon only looked at her husband with a shocked expression on her face. At last she opened her mouth to speak, but Mrs. Carlyle cut her off.

"Well, it worked!" the maid blurted out. She pointed at the line of people who had shown up to vote before turning to Oona. "Look at this turnout. Not everything I said was a lie. I do want Molly Morgana Moon on the Dark Street Council. It's time women's voices are heard."

Oona frowned at her. "But not the voice of a lying, deceitful woman like you."

"Well said," Molly Morgana Moon agreed.

The inspector took Mrs. Carlyle by the wrist and led her forcefully toward the back of the police carriage.

"Where did you find Denis Carlyle, Inspector?" Oona asked.

"Where they were staying, at the Nightshade Hotel,"

he said before giving Oona a pompous look. "I told you we have our ways of finding people, Miss Crate."

Oona was quite impressed.

The inspector reached into his coat pocket and pulled out a small leather-bound book. "Oh, I found this in their room. It's full of magical gibberish. Looks to be the book she stole from Pendulum House."

"It certainly is," said Samuligan. He put out his hand and the inspector handed the book over.

"By the way, where is the carbuncle?" the inspector asked.

"It is here," Samuligan said. He held up the glimmering ruby.

The inspector put out his hand expectantly, but the faerie did not hand the gem over.

"We shall find a safe place for it," the Wizard said. "Samuligan will keep it for now."

The inspector shrugged, as if it did not matter to him. He continued to direct Mrs. Carlyle to the back of the wagon.

Oona felt a tightening in her chest as Mrs. Carlyle was shoved into the carriage and the doors were slammed shut. She could hear the husband and wife begin to argue through the bars.

"I told you not to tie up the night watchman with that bloody knot of yours," Mr. Carlyle said in a piercing voice. "It's always caused nothing but attention."

"Oh, shut your mouth, Denis!" Mrs. Carlyle snapped back. "You're the one who gambled all the money away."

"Oh, so it's all my fault, is it?" Mr. Carlyle said indignantly.

"Back to the station," the inspector called as he climbed back onto the high passenger seat. "If we hurry up and book them now, I might have time to vote before the polls close. Tallyho!"

The constable snapped the reins, and Oona watched the carriage swing around in the street and head north toward police headquarters. A whirlwind of emotions collided in her as she watched them go. There was relief and satisfaction at knowing that her father's killers were finally captured and put behind bars...and yet there was also a strange kind of emptiness the came over her. It was something she had not expected. The fact that the culprits were finally being brought to justice seemed to do nothing to fill the space her father's death had left behind...and presently she wondered if anything would ever fill it.

Behind her, Samuligan helped the Wizard out of the carriage. A moment later the two of them joined Oona, and together they watched her father's killers being taken to jail. Her uncle's comforting hand rested on her shoulder.

"Well, in light of these unforeseen events," the Wizard said, "I would say that your final battle test is unnecessary."

Oona looked up at him, surprised. "Really?"

The Wizard winked. "This was a far more rigorous test than I would have conceived. You handled a real situation against someone with faerielike powers. And I would say you passed with all flags flying."

Oona peered down at the feather in her hand. It was no longer white as it had been when connected with Oswald's wand, and it had returned to its previous shade of midnight black.

"Oswald's wand," Oona said. "It connected with the feather and was destroyed."

The Wizard peered thoughtfully at the feather, scratching at his beard. "Of that, I have no answers. It is magic on a grand and mysterious level."

Oona sighed heavily. "The wand destroyed my father's magnifying glass. It exploded...and this time I think it's gone for good."

The glass had been her dearest possession, and the loss was profound. She recalled the time Isadora Iree carelessly tossed it across the room and the glass had shattered, and how she, Oona, had uttered the incantation to mend the glass like new. She had uttered the spell on instinct during a time when she had sworn off ever doing magic again—so important had the magnifying glass been to her. But in that event it had been only the glass that had shattered. Now the entire thing had been destroyed, blown into hundreds, maybe even thousands of pieces and particles all over the street. It was beyond magical repair.

They were all quiet for a long moment, each lost in their own thoughts, when at last the silence was broken.

"This is going to be my first published critique!"

They all turned to discover Mary Shusher standing at the edge of the sidewalk with her mother on one side and her father on the other.

"I saw the whole thing," Mary said excitedly, "and I just can't wait to write about it."

She held up a writing pad and a fancy-looking fountain pen that looked to Oona as if it were made out of pearl.

"Oh, hello there," Oona said, sounding less than enthusiastic. Realizing that both mother and daughter were there together, she asked: "Who's tending to the library today?"

"It's closed on the weekends," came the lilting voice of Adler Iree.

At first Oona did not see him. She looked quickly around and found him hurrying toward her from across the street, a look of concern on his tattooed face. "I heard there was some sort of magic happening down the street, and I figured you must be involved." He cast his gaze about the wreckage. "Are you all right?"

"I'm fine," Oona said, and as happy as she was to see Adler, she did not feel much like explaining everything that had happened. She felt exhausted.

Luckily, Mr. Shusher took that moment to step forward and distract her.

"I owe you an apology, Miss Crate," he said stiffly, "for how I reacted to your questions on the library steps the other day. You see, I have heard about your detective business, and I was under the impression that you and Mary were friends, and that she had asked you to find out what her birthday present was. I knew that you had overheard Mrs. Shusher and me speaking of hiding it, and I did not want to give you any more information."

"Oh, that's what you were talking about hiding," Oona said, and then in order to break the highly awkward silence that followed, she asked. "And what did you get, Mary?"

"I got exactly what I wanted. This expensive new fountain pen," Mary boasted, and held it up so that its opalescent surface glinted in the sunlight. "And I'm going to use it to write reviews. You see, Mother has finally relented, and is willing to let me try my hand as a professional reviewer. It turns out that she is a friend of the head editor at the *Dark Street Tribune*. They are going to give me a column to write my reviews, once a week to start with, but if people find my critiques helpful it could expand to a daily. I'll be an actual staff writer." Mary squeezed her mother's arm.

"Congratulations," Deacon said enthusiastically. "That makes you the first female writer the *Tribune* has ever hired."

"Bravo!" said Molly Morgana Moon. "That is a wonderful achievement. Tell me, what will you be writing about for your first article?"

Mary was practically beaming. "Well, I wasn't quite sure until just a few moments ago, but now I know exactly what it will be." She turned to Oona, her eyes full of excitement. "I'm going to write about what everyone will be talking about tomorrow. Your magical battle. Isn't that exciting?"

Adler stifled a laugh as Oona's lips tightened peevishly.

"That's just...wonderful," Oona said through a phony smile, and then, wishing to get away from all of the attention, she turned to Adler. "I have something I want to show you."

Taking him by the hand, she led him around the other

side of the carriage. Her heart was all at once pounding in her chest like a fist against a door.

"Deacon, may we have a minute?" Oona asked.

"Certainly," Deacon said, sounding more than happy to give them space as he took to the air and disappeared over the carriage.

"I need to ask you something," Oona said.

Adler looked nervous, which in turn made Oona feel even more nervous than she already did. But it did not matter. She had already made up her mind to ask the question.

"Okay," Adler said. "What is it?"

"Will you be my boyfriend?" she asked.

A long pause followed, in which the sound of Oona's beating heart filled the entire world.

At last Adler smiled so broadly that the tattooed moons at the corners of his eyes crinkled slightly.

"I thought you'd never ask," he said.

Oona was taken aback. "Me? But...I thought—"

"That it was the boy's job?" he finished for her. "I know...but I told Isadora that I was going to ask you last month. But she said that the modern girl wants to ask the boy." He looked thoughtful. "Then again, that was just after she and Roderick broke up. That might have been a bad time to take her advice."

Oona shook her head. "Take it from me, don't listen to Isadora when it comes to love."

"Love?" Adler said.

Oona's face flushed as red as a barn. "I mean to say...um..."

Adler gave her hand a squeeze. "I think I know what you mean."

Oona cleared her throat. "Is that a yes?"

"Is *what* a yes?" Adler asked.

Oona gave him a calculating look. "You know, the whole boyfriend thing."

"Oh," Adler said, and then tipped his hat. "Yes, of course."

Oona finally allowed herself to smile. She felt tired but happy, and it seemed that perhaps a tiny part of that emptiness she had felt earlier was suddenly filled up—not completely, not by a long shot, but a part of it...and that, she knew, was a start.

"What's that?' Adler asked curiously, pointing at the feather in Oona's hand.

"Oh, this?" Oona said. She held the feather up by the tip and spun it between her fingers. "It's a key."

She did not know why she said it, but the instant she did, she knew it was the truth. It felt right.

"A key to what?" Adler asked.

She nearly replied: "To my heart." But instead, she simply said: "That is a mystery for another day."

Chapter Fifteen

Feather of Crow

They met in secret. In the cemetery. Unchaperoned.

The boy waited for her just inside the arched stone entrance. He was reading the newspaper, and when Oona saw him, she smiled.

"Hello, Adler."

"Hello, Oona."

Adler folded the newspaper, picked up the picnic basket, and placed the paper on top.

The fact that he had used her first name did not escape her. She took his hand, and the two of them began to make their way across the hilly grounds of the graveyard. The sun was bright overhead, yet the morning mist still hovered stubbornly several inches thick above the ground.

"No Deacon?" Adler asked, glancing toward Oona's shoulder.

"I left him at home," Oona said. "Samuligan drove me here, but he's waiting at the curb. He thinks I'm alone."

"I'll bet he's not fooled," Adler said.

Oona shrugged and looked at the paper on the basket. "I see you have the *Tribune*. I take it you read about Molly Morgana Moon's victory over Tobias Fink."

"I did," he said. "It was a close race, and they counted the votes five times, but in the end, she won."

Oona shook her head, and Adler raised an eyebrow.

"I thought you'd be pleased," Adler said. "She's the first female Dark Street Council member ever."

"Oh, I'm happy about that. It's just the *way* that she won that I don't like. If it wasn't for Mrs. Carlyle and her husband's riot, Molly Morgana Moon might never have gotten elected."

Adler nodded. "Aye. Things have a funny way of working out, so they do."

"What do you mean?" Oona asked.

"Well, it's just that Mrs. Carlyle was so concerned about getting a woman elected, she didn't think about the fact that one of Molly Morgana Moon's main promises was to cut crime on the street. That would never have worked in Mrs. Carlyle's favor, being that she was a criminal herself."

Oona frowned. "But that's just the thing. It was from Mrs. Carlyle that I learned the value of women's rights. I had never even considered such matters before she came to work at Pendulum House. And now it turns out she was a horrible person. She and her husband killed my father."

Adler suddenly stopped walking and stared at the ground, apparently thinking hard. Finally, he looked up at her and asked: "Do you think it's possible that people are not completely good or bad? I mean, you just said it yourself that this despicable woman showed you something that you believe is good."

"That's what makes it so confusing," Oona said. "She's a thief and a killer, and yet..." Oona did not want to finish the sentence. She felt guilty and wrong for thinking it.

"And yet she taught you something important," Adler finished for her, and shrugged. "Like I said, things have a funny way of working out."

Oona sighed, and the two of them started walking again, moving toward the far end of the cemetery, where

Oona had some business to attend to. To their right, the enormous seven-hundred-foot-tall Black Tower jutted out of the graveyard like an enormous tombstone. Inside those solid black walls lived a group of card-playing goblins. Oona recalled how she had ridden to the top of that dark tower in a rowboat fastened to a hot-air balloon. What an adventure that had been. But it was not the goblins she was planning on visiting today, and she could feel her nerves beginning to flutter like hummingbird wings in her stomach.

"Of course, you made the paper, too," Adler said. "That's what I was reading when you got here."

"Yes, Samuligan told me," Oona said. "I haven't read it."

Adler looked surprised. "Why not?"

Oona shrugged. "Because I lived it. I remember what happened quite well."

"Oh, I see," Adler said.

Oona blushed slightly. "I was going to read it...but before I turned to the review page, Deacon quoted a famous theater director to me—a man named Robert Gristle Wistlesnap—who said that if you believe the good reviews, then you must believe the bad ones as well. So...I decided to leave it be."

Adler cocked an eyebrow. "You believe that, about the good ones and the bad ones?"

Again Oona shrugged, unsure what she believed. She looked curiously at the newspaper folded on the picnic basket.

Adler grinned at her and wriggled his eyebrows. "You sure you don't want to know?"

Oona half grinned back. "I suppose I am curious, but..."

Adler picked the paper up, waving it playfully in front of her. "She was actually quite flattering toward you, Mary Shusher was."

"Was she?" Oona said, surprised.

"Oh, aye," Adler said. "She wrote something about magic becoming fashionable again because of you."

"Because of me?" Oona said, and snatched the newspaper from Adler's hand. "Let me see."

Adler laughed. "What happened to: 'If you believed the good ones, then you need to believe the bad?'"

Oona shook her head. "Oh, rubbish! Let's see. Ah, here it is. 'Wizard's Apprentice Wows Crowd in Vivacious Show of Magic.'" She frowned.

"What's the matter?" Adler asked.

Oona folded the paper and handed it back without reading any further. She sighed. "It's nice, yes. But the thing is, I wasn't putting on a show. I was fighting for my life."

Adler nodded thoughtfully. "Aye. I suppose that's true, so it is."

He once again took Oona's hand and gave it a squeeze. Oona squeezed back and tried to put the newspaper article out of her mind. She had business to attend to.

At last, the two of them crested a hill, and below them, spread out in a square patch of earth, was what they had walked all this way to see. It was the Crate family plot, the place where her mother and sister and father all lay in their final resting places. Oona had not been here in more than three years. She took in an extra deep breath to steady her nerves.

"Will you give me a moment?" she asked.

"Of course," Adler said, and released her hand.

Oona started forward, but paused and looked back. "I'm glad you came with me."

Adler gave her a tip of his hat, and then his eyes moved to the cemetery plot beyond. Oona turned, and soon her feet led her to the three headstones farthest along the plot. She read the familiar names. Her eyes were dry, despite the whirlwind of emotions that filled her. Her instincts told her what to do.

Slowly, Oona touched her fingers to her lips, and then

one by one placed the kiss upon the three tombstones. As she did so, she felt a strange kind of awareness come over her: an awareness of someone watching her. She knew Adler was watching, but he was at a distance. This feeling was of someone very near.

Slowly, she pulled the black feather from her pocket and held it up before the third tombstone: the one with her father's name upon it.

"Thank you, Father," she said. "I miss you." She looked toward her mother's tombstone, and her sister Flora's. "I miss all of you."

For the briefest of moments, Oona felt a hand touch her own. It was a familiar touch, the same hand she had felt when it had handed her the feather in the dream cemetery, one she had known her entire life. Oona gasped as she turned her attention back to her father's tombstone, only to discover that her hand was empty. The feather was gone.

Oona stared at her empty hand for a long time. She had somehow known that this is what would happen, and yet it was a surprise all the same.

When at last she turned to go, she looked up the hill at Adler, who was watching her curiously.

"What's that?" he asked, gesturing toward the ground.

Oona looked down to see what he was pointing at, and that's when she saw it, lying in the misty grass upon her father's grave: Oswald's wand! It would have been impossible to mistake.

Oona picked it up out of the thinning mist, her face filled with astonishment.

"But wasn't that destroyed?" Adler asked.

Oona nodded. She had seen it disintegrate before her eyes. And then she remembered. "Its power went into the feather. Into my father's feather."

Adler walked to join her. "What does it mean?"

"It means," Oona said with a shiver, "that the key to the Glass Gates still exists. Everyone else thinks it's been destroyed, and now we're the only ones who know about it."

"Oh," Adler said thoughtfully, and then put out his hand. "Well, put it away then." He held up the basket. "I'm getting hungry, and I'd like to have a picnic with my girlfriend, if she doesn't mind."

Oona smiled and tucked the wand into her dress pocket. "You know...she doesn't mind at all."

She took his hand and the two of them ventured over the hill and beyond. The day was full of possibilities and mysteries to discover.

Behind them, like vigilant guardians in the dispersing mist, the three tombstones stood silent and watchful, reflecting sunlight off their polished surfaces as an afternoon breeze blew through the Dark Street Cemetery, whirling and dancing like a whisper of song and illusion, and a promise of dreams to come.

About The Author

Shawn Thomas Odyssey is the Edgar- and Agatha-Award nominated author of the *Oona Crate Mysteries*, which include *The Wizard of Dark Street* and *The Magician's Tower*. When he isn't writing novels, he is a professional music composer of films and TV, with works including HBO's *Deadwood*.

For more Dark Street fun visit
www.shawnthomasodyssey.com.

Don't miss these other exciting Oona Crate mysteries!

The Wizard of Dark Street (book 1)
The Magician's Tower (book 2)
—

Also by Shawn Thomas Odyssey

The Monster Society

—

All books available as audiobooks from
audible.com

CPSIA information can be obtained
at www.ICGtesting.com
Printed in the USA
LVOW13s1127270517
536042LV00013BA/195/P